Gustav

Gustav

GRAHAM PRATT

authorHOUSE®

AuthorHouse™
1663 Liberty Drive
Bloomington, IN 47403
www.authorhouse.com
Phone: 1-800-839-8640

Published by AuthorHouse   03/21/2012

ISBN: 978-1-4678-9615-3 (sc)
ISBN: 978-1-4678-9616-0 (e)

THE CALM BEFORE
THE STORM

WESTHAMPTON IS THE quintessential English village. The main road through the village consisted of the Red Lion Pub, The Old Tea Shoppe, the village school, and St Mark's Church. There was a right turn before you came to the village, which passed by Wright's farm and three miles further on was the old Manor House.

Robert Thomas who was a high ranking local government officer employed by the Council. He was in his mid thirties and had black hair which was now showing signs of grey just at the sides. He had purchased one of the new houses on a private housing Estate in the village. He like the other villagers had seen the restoration work going on at the Manor, but only he and a few others through their contacts knew the names of the new owners.

The old Manor house was three miles down Manor Lane after you passed by Wright's Farm. The entrance to the Manor was along a crescent shaped drive way, which led to the grand imposing front door. Some local tradesmen were restoring some stained glass in the two large doors, which separated the porch from the grand hall. In the stained glass was a coat of arms a black shield upon which was a red castle. Underneath the shield was the family's name Rothenburg.

It all happened one Monday morning a removal van pulled up outside the Red Lion about nine o'clock. The driver went in and asked Joe the landlord for directions to the manor. The Red Lion was your typical village Pub. It had stone floors, wooden beams. The lounge bar was for functions and parties. Most of the locals drank in the vaults where you did not need to dress up but could go in your working clothes.

About noon a big black Daimler pulled up outside the Old Tea Shoppe, and a middle aged couple got out to stretch their legs followed by a young man with blond hair who was in his mid twenties. The young man entered the Shop. And asked Gloria Brown the owner how to get to the Manor. She noticed his accent despite perfect English He pronounced it Vesthampton not Westhampton. Gloria was a friendly person, but a notorious gossip. She could not wait to spread the news of the encounter with a young blond foreigner.

At five o'clock the removal van came back into the village and the men went into the Red Lion for a drink after a hard day's work. They went into the vaults and began to tell Joe that the Rothenburgs must have a bob or two judging on the expensive furniture which they had just unloaded from the van. In the vaults were two of the locals Fred Wright a farmer in his fifties. He was a stocky man and had a red face because he worked in the open air. His drinking partner was Colonel Price-waters retired, who was your stereotype ex military man. He had a small mustache and he always wore his blazer with its regimental badge on it.

When they heard the name of the new owners. Fred said "Rothenburg that sounds foreign to me" Robert Thomas had just finished work in the municipal offices and on hearing the conversation. He could now reveal all. The Rothenburgs are a old German family from Bad Rothenburg. They made their wealth in the wine business the family consist of Helmut Rothenburg the father, Hildegard the mother and their son Gustav Leopold Rothenburg. In fact I have just come in for a quick drink before the parish councillors and I go to the Manor to the welcome the family to the village. Robert said. Then one of the other councillors came into the pub and informed Robert it was time to go to the Manor House. They drove in a convoy of cars down Manor lane and drove into the drive way and parked their cars in the parking places. Then they went up to the large wooden front door and rang the bell. The doors was opened by a elderly man with grey hair. Robert Was soon to come to know this was Gerhardt a faithful family servant. He asked them what they wanted and Robert acting as spokesman for the party informed him who they were and that they had come to welcome the Rothenburgs to the village. Gerhardt showed them in through the large double doors that separated the porch from the grand hall. They noticed the coat of arms in the stained glass windows. The grand hall was wood panelled and in front of them was a grand staircase. On the walls were portraits of Helmut, Hildegard and Gustav Leopold Rothenburg. They were shown into the drawing room. It had a large dining table and chairs near the fireplace were red chesterfield armchairs and a settee. There were French windows leading out onto the terrace and gardens below. After a few minutes the door opened and entered a young man in his mid twenties. Robert guessed that he was about five foot eleven and weighed around twelve stones. He had blond hair and piercing blue eyes. He was wearing a light blue shirt, and white flannels. Robert could not miss the expensive gold rolex wristwatch. The young man introduced himself as Gustav Rothenburg. He was the accountant for the family's wine business. Robert soon noticed that Gustav expected people to act with deference towards him and was put out if they did not. Gustav had a superior attitude about him. But Robert was soon to learn that Gustav was a shy young man when you got to know him and this was just his defence system. Soon Robert and Gustav would become firm friends. Robert and the councillors were given a quick tour of the downstairs of the Manor from the Drawing room you entered the grand ballroom by way of two large doors. The ball room had elaborate ceilings and large gilt chandeliers. The room had dark blue velvet curtains which were not just for show, but also to keep the cold out. Again French windows led out onto the terrace and gardens. When you came out of the drawing room to one side was Gustav's office. At one side of the grand staircase was the door to the family's private living room used only by the family and their close circle of friends as Robert was to find out. The other side of the staircase was the swimming pool and the servants quarters. Robert knew that Gustav would need someone in the village to help him avoid clashes with the locals.

Some days later Robert invited Gustav to come to the Red Lion and meet some of the Locals. Robert introduced Gustav to Joe the landlord saying "Hello Joe come and meet the new lord of the Manor Gustav Rothenburg. Well in the vaults bar there were two of the locals Fred Wright and Colonel Price-Waters and on hearing the name. They were curious and not to put to fine a point on it nosy. So they came into the lounge bar. By now Gustav and Robert were having a meal and a drink. Robert saw them coming and introduced Gustav to them. Gustav nodded and continued eating his meal. Fred Wright and the colonel were clearly expecting him to say something. But he just looked at them with his piercing blue eyes. The colonel finally said "you are a arrogant beggar. I have heard tales of goose stepping German officers in the second world war just like you." Gustav laughed and said "I wondered how long it would be before you mentioned the war" I am only in my twenties so I was not in it." but some of you British people will not forget it." The Colonel said "you and your family think you are going to run this village don't you". "but you are a arrogant young man, who do you think you are. The Kaiser. "Well no sooner had the colonel said it The Kaiser became Gustav's nickname in the village because of his superior manner when you first met him. The door of the lounge bar opened and a chauffeur came in. Gustav said "ah hello Heinrich". Then turning to Robert he thanked him and Joe for the meal and the drink. He looked at fred Wright and the Colonel and said that he looked forward to meeting them again but had another meeting and had to go. He stood erect and nodded goodbye saying to the chauffeur "Heinrich nach hause bitte" Henry home please. As the chauffeur opened the door of the Daimler to let Gustav get in.

The Colonel said "well I almost expected him to click his heels together." Fred and the colonel both agreed that Gustav was going to upset quite a few of the locals. Robert laughed as he walked home he knew that Gustav needed the help of someone to guide him through the minefield that village life could be. And fortunately he knew just the person.

Ms Friday Jane Wright had just qualified with a business degree, but so far had no success in finding employment even though she had tried looking in the nearest large town to Westhampton. Jane was attractive with black hair. She had her father's wit and her mother's warmth of heart. So Robert told her that he knew of someone who needed a personal assistant and would she be interested. She agreed to go with Robert that afternoon. He picked up her at the farmhouse. She was now wearing her black business suit and carrying a document case containing her cv and qualifications. But Robert did not drive towards the nearest large town. He drove further along Manor Lane. And then turned into the entrance to the Manor. They parked the car and Robert knocked at the door, which was opened as usual by Gerhardt. Robert told him that they had aappointment with Gustav. He showed them into the grand hall. Jane noticed the coat of arms and the portraits especially Gustsav's. He had them wait while he knocked on Gustav's office door and went in. Soon he ushered them in. Gustav was behind his p c. When he saw Robert he got up and came to shake his hand. Jane noticed that they acted more than just friends. Robert introduced Jane to Gustav. She opened her document case showed him her cv and qualifications. The office was small but well equipped there was a desk and pc for her. A fax machine and a machine for photocopying documents. The interview went well and Gustav offered Jane the job. So he invited them into the drawing room and asked Gerhardt to bring in some coffee and tea and biscuits. They sat in the red chestferfield furniture near the fire. Jane noticed Gustav's superior manner which had so offended her father. But she warmed to this young German. Jane soon found another friend at the Manor. Hildegard liked to catch up on the local gossip. So she invited Jane into the living room and explained that back home in bad Rothenburg she would invite friends around for kaffee und kuchen tea and cakes and share the local gossip. Jane mentioned the old tea shoppe and how Gloria Brown the owner knew all the local gossip but her homemade cakes were wonderful. So it was agreed that next Wednesday they would go to the old tea shoppe and Gustav would have to come with them. On Wednesday afternoon the Daimler pulled up outside the old tea shoppe. Heinrich opened the doors so that they all could get out. They went inside the shop Gloria was delighted to see the handsome young stranger again. She ushered them to a table in a corner. The old tea shoppe is a tourist delight with crisp white tablecloths and as if by magic when they sat down cake stands full of homemade cakes appeared. Soon Hildegard and Jane were getting on like a house on fire. Hildegard mentioned how as a child Gustav would go into the kitchen for Strawberry Gateau with whipped cream. Jane knew that Gloria made a Strawberry Gateau to die for. So she ordered three portions with whipped cream of course. Jane soon worked out that it was Gustav's Achilles heel that if you wanted to get him somewhere you just mentioned that there would be homemade cream cakes there. When the strawberry gateau arrived Gustav was like a child again. Then Hildegard told Jane that back home in Bad Rothenburg Gustav and his friends would ride around the country lanes on old rusty bicycles. Jane could not believe it looking at Gustav in his Ralph lauren or Hugo Boss outfits. Hi m riding a old rusty bicycle. But then Hildegard told jane a story that did ring true. As a child if he and his friends were playing soldiers Gustav had to be the general and quite often some of the other boys would come in crying because Gustav would not let them take turns in being the general. No change there then thought Jane. Gustav said that he had to go to another meeting. But that he would have Heinrich take them back to the Manor and have him pick Gustav up later. Jane knew that Gustav was going to the Red Lion for a drink with Robert Thomas in the lounge bar. Her father Fred drank in the vaults and had seen them there together what her father called Robert's audience with the Kaiser.

THE OPEN DAY

It was at one of Gustav's and Robert's weekly gatherings in the lounge bar of the Red Lion. These gatherings Fred Wright called Robert's audience with the Kaiser. Gustav and Robert always had the same table in a corner of the Lounge. From there they could see everyone who came into the lounge bar. Robert's idea was for a open day at the Manor House. The Rothenburgs had been in Westhampton for nearly a month now, But there were still some people who had not met them and seen the improvements they had made to the Manor. Robert suggested that the Manor be open to the public from nine in the morning until four in the afternoon Gustav thought it was a splendid idea. So he had Jane have some posters printed and placed around the village. Visitors would be able to partake of drinks and a buffet. So Fred and the Colonel agreed to come and have a look around the restored Manor.

They drove up to the Manor and entered the drive way. They parked in a reserved parking place and went up to the imposing front door, and rang the bell the door was opened by Gerhardt, who showed them in. Past the two large wooden doors which divided the porch from the grand hall. They noticed the Rothenburg coat of arms in the stained glass. They stood for a while in the large hall with it's wood paneled walls and the grand stair case in front of them. They saw the portraits of the family on the walls especially Gustav's. To the right of the entrance was Gustav's office and then the drawing room. To one side of the stairs was the door to the family's living room, which the public was not allowed to enter to the left of the stairs was the swimming pool and the door to the staff quarters and kitchen and laundry. The garage was at the rear of the Manor. Fred and the Colonel entered the drawing room. The room had a large dining table and chairs. The ceilings had ornate chandeliers. There were red chesterfield furniture near to the fireplace. To one side of the room there were tables heavily laden with food and wine. The wine bottles had a label on them showing the Rothenburg coat of arms. The wine had come from Uncle Ernst vineyard in Bad Rothenburg near Koblenz. "Snobbish sods" expressed Fred Wright and the Colonel. But they had to admit it was good German plonk. From the drawing room the French windows led out onto the terrace and gardens. In the distance was the river which was the boundary of the Rothenburg estate. The family used the drawing room as a reception room. From the drawing room two large doors led into the grand ballroom. This was an imposing room The gilt chandeliers along it's length and The elaborate plaster work on it. The room had dark blue velvet curtains and not just for show, But to keep the cold out. French windows led out onto the terrace and gardens. The guide explained that the family liked to have their breakfast on the terrace on warm sunny mornings. "Not bad for some" muttered Fred.

They came back into the hall and then up the grand stair case passed Gustav's portrait which Fred blew a raspberry at. The guide showed them some of the bedrooms, But not those used by the family. All the rooms had a four poster bed, and all had ensuite facilities. Large windows looked out onto the village countryside. The guide explained that Gustav's room had a walk in wardrobe where they hanged his clothes once they had been washed and ironed. Fred jokingly asked if he washed and ironed them himself. The guide was horrified "Master Gustav does not wash or iron his own clothes" Fred snorted "pampered mummy's boy". They came back down the grand staircase and sat out on the terrace admiring the gardens." Fred said "I would be a snob like the Kaiser if I lived here as well" They both laughed. They had to admit the Rothenburg's had brought the Manor back to it's pristine glory.

After the open day was over Robert and Gustav and the rest of the family celebrated with a relaxing drink in the family's living room to toast the day's success. The men had brandy while Hildegard and Jane had sweet sherry. The locals could now see the hard work the family had put in to restoring the Manor. But Fred and the Colonel and the other people in the village who did not get on with the Rothenburgs only backed up their ideas that the family had bid ideas about themselves and loved to let others know just how well off they were.

THE FUND RAISING EVENT

GLORIA BROWN HAD been one of the visitors around the Manor and it had given her an idea. On Monday afternoon there was the meeting of the St Mark's fund raising committee held as normal in the Church Hall and chaired by the vicar Rev Jeremy Browne. The main topic was the annual fair to raise funds for the restoration fund. Gloria suggested why did they not ask the Rothenburgs if they would permit the Church to hold the event in the grounds of the Manor. She said that she was quite willing to ask Gustav. Gloria fancied Gustav and all the village was aware of it. Rev Jeremy Browne was unsure he had heard tales of others facing the acid tongue of Gustav Rothenburg and did not want to see Gloria upset. But the meeting thought that the idea should be investigated.

Next morning Gloria came across Jane Wright Gustav's PA on the high street. But not by chance oh no not on

Gloria's part. Gloria outlined the idea to Jane who said that she could not give her a definite answer there and then, But she would put the suggestion before Gustav that day and let Gloria know the outcome. Jane drove to the Manor house and parked her mini in her reserved place at the front of the Manor. Gustav was on the terrace finishing his breakfast. He offered Jane a cup of coffee before they started work. Jane seized the moment and put the suggestion to Gustav about how St Mark's Church wanted to use the Manor House gardens for their annual fair to raise money for the restoration fund. She mentioned it was Gloria's idea. Gustav thought for a moment it would allow the people in the village to see what the Manor had to offer for weddings and so on. He agreed and he and Jane thought that the Church could have a exhibition in the ballroom showing how the restoration fund was growing. So Jane phoned Gloria in the old Tea Shoppe with the good news the event was on.

Jane had posters printed and displayed around the village. They saw one of the posters outside the Red Lion. In the vaults the Colonel was furious" that scheming german git" He does not care about St Marks He is only doing this to spread his family's influence in the village. It's not for the Church it's for the Rothenburgs. Joe the landlord had heard it all before "business as usual" he sighed.

On the Saturday morning of the fair Gustav was woken by Gerhardt at seven in the morning as usual with his cup of coffee. Gustav showered and dressed. Then came down the grand stair case and had breakfast on the terrace with the rest of the family. Jane arrived at nine in the morning. To help arrange the tables and chairs on the terrace for guests to sit down and enjoy their drinks. There was a large marquee in the grounds which was the beer tent run by the Red Lion. Other marquees and other tents were being set up for the mother's union with their homemade cakes, jams, chutneys in the other tents were stalls and games for the children.

When the fair was open Gustav visited the Mother's union stall with it's homemade cakes Cream cakes were Gustav's Achilles heel. The Mother's union marquee was near to the beer tent. So Fred and the Colonel could hear the ladies saying how handsome Gustav was and how charming. And how much he appreciated their cakes." Fred shouted "Joe can you bring me a bucket I'm going to be sick. Listening to them old biddies butt kissing that kraut". It got worse for Fred later on from the beer tent you could see Gustav and Robert laughing and joking with the local councillors on the terrace sipping Rothenburg sparkling wine. The Colonel said "you cannot see the leader of the council because he is so far up Gustav's arse" "all you can see are his boots". Fred carried on "it's not because he is german Helmut and Hildegard are lovely people but him the Kaiser with his airs and graces. He just rubs me up the wrong way lording it over us." Then the public address system announced That this year the Children's fancy dress would be judged by Mr Gustav Rothenburg. The Colonel laughed "He'll pick the one that's dressed as the Kaiser" Fred and the others laughed.

The exhibition was in the ballroom. The stands showed photographs and plans of the project. How much money was needed and how much they had raised so far. Helmut, Hildegard, and Gustav were standing with the vicar looking at the photographs. Hildegard told the vicar that back home the prettiest stretch of the Rhine was from Koblenz to Rudesheim. Bad Rothenburg was just outside Koblenz. It was a small village just like Westhampton. But that the family had always gone to Church on Sunday morning." Rev Jeremy Browne was delighted he invited them to come to the morning worship. Hildegard said on behalf of all the family that they would be delighted. The vicar knew this would be a feather in his cap when the bishop heard how he had managed to get the new owners of the restored manor to come to Church.

Gustav looked rueful the thought of sitting on a rock hard pew for an hour did not fill him with joy. The fair had been a great success. Gloria was relieved because it had been a big gamble for her and she had got to be near Gustav. The family were pleased because the villagers had the chance to see what the Manor had to offer for weddings and other functions. When all the villagers had gone home. The family and their close circle of friends withdrew into their private quarters. They relaxed in the chesterfield furniture toasting their success with champagne. Hildegard said that they should have more events like these to show people in the village that the Rothenburgs only wanted to be part of the village. The rest agreed.

MORNING WORSHIP
AT ST MARKS

Sunday started as every day for Gustav. He was woken up by Gerhardt at seven with his cup of coffee. Then Gustav showered and dressed. But today the family were attending morning worship for the first time at St Marks. Gustav selected his black hugo boss business suit it always made the right impression. He wore a freshly ironed white shirt and wore a silk tie. He wore his gold cufflinks which had his initials engraved on them. And to finish of the outfit he wore black shoes and socks.

The family had breakfast on the terrace Heinrich brought the Daimler around to the front of the House at quarter past ten. The service was not until eleven o'clock Helmut, Hildegard got into the car first followed by Gustav. The Daimler soon arrived at the Church. It was your stereotype village Church. It had a Lych gate with a wall

all around and there were yew trees in the grounds. Fred Wright and the Colonel were waiting outside the pub to go in. When the saw the car they knew the family must be going to Church. Fred and The Colonel waved when Helmut and Hildegard got out. Then they saw Gustav. The Colonel said "he will never get his big head through the door, and he will be all day in confession". Fred Wright spoke loud enough for Gustav to hear. "one of the commandments must be thou shalt not be a big headed German twat". Gustav was walking up the path with Helmut and Hildegard before him. He stopped clearly going to turn round and give them a mouthful. Hildegard knew her son and she knew what he was going to do. This was Sunday morning and she did not want him embarrassing her. So she said in that tone of voice only a mother can use when she wants to reprimand her wayward child. "Gustav Leopold come on" Gustav replied "ja mutti" yes mum. Fred and the colonel laughed to see the Kaiser pulled back into line so easily.

Inside the Church. It was in a cruciform shape. The altar was at the top. The transept formed the beam of the cross. The nave the base of the cross. The pulpit was to the left of the altar with the lectern in the form of a eagle to the right. Near the altar were pews for the choir. Behind the altar was a stained glass window of Christ the light of the world by Holman Hunt. The Font was at the entrance of the Church. The verger led the family to the pews near the front. There was no reserved pew here for the lords of the Manor. But the congregation chatted excitedly when they saw the family.

The vicar Rev Jeremy Browne was a kind man in his fifties. He looked born to be a clergyman. He had silver grey hair and metal rimmed spectacles. He started the service by welcoming the family to his flock. And said the first hymn was by Martin Luther "ein feste burg" a safe stronghold is our God because it reminded him of the Rothenburg coat of arms which had a castle on it. And he was glad to see the village had made the family welcome. But Gustav could not get comfortable. The pews were hard. And he gazed around the Church and the congregation much to Hildegard's annoyance. She gave him a swift dig in the ribs to remember where he was and why. The choir sang an anthem. But thankfully the sermon was not a long one. Soon the service was over. The congregation came up and shook their hands. Gloria was the secretary for the Mother's union and when she got hold of Gustav's hand she seemed not to want to let it go. The family thanked the vicar for his service and Hildegard said that they had all enjoyed it and would be back next week. Gustav managed a smile and shook the vicar's hand.

Then the bit Gustav was looking forward to. They had arranged to meet Robert in the Red Lion for Sunday lunch. He had told them that the Sunday roast dinner Joe made was wonderful. So the family walked through the lych gate and across the road to the pub. Robert was there already he had reserved a table. Joe saw Gustav and his parents come in. Fred and the Colonel had been warned by Joe the landlord to leave Gustav alone at least while his parents were with him. Or else they would be barred. They all ordered the traditional Sunday lunch of roast beef and all the trimmings which the Rothenburgs had to admit was first class. The meal was washed down with some cask beer for the men, and Hildegard had red wine. The family were pleased to see that the wine was a Rothenburg wine which Gustav had sold Joe at a good discount For dessert they had apple pie with cream. Joe ever the perfect host came to their table to make sure that everything was alright. They thanked Joe for the lovely meal. Fred and the Colonel smiled at Gustav from the other bar. Gustav knew that they were up to something and that it would involve him.

The family relaxed in the comfy chairs after their hearty meal which had been washed down with a couple of pints each of cask ale. And two glasses of red wine for Hildegard. Before they knew it. Heinrich was at the door waiting to take them home. Robert had walked. So Gustav offered him a lift home. Fred and the Colonel said goodbye to Gustav. Both Joe and Gustav looked at each other and at them, but they said they had done nothing wrong only said goodbye. Joe was not convinced. But he was glad the family had enjoyed their meal and hoped that they would come again next Sunday lunch.

CLASH OF THE TITANS

ROBERT THOMAS REMEMBERED the meeting of the tourism sub committee at which Gustav's name came up to be co-0pted onto the committee as a advisor. Most of the committee agreed except for Councillor Maggie Pettigrew or Red Maggie as Robert referred to her behind her back. The Rothenburgs represented everything she hated privilege, class distinction, and most of all wealth. She disliked the reputation Gustav had acquired around the village. His nickname of the Kaiser because of his superior attitude and how he expected people to act with deference towards him. But the meeting agreed to invite Gustav to the next meeting.

The morning of the meeting arrived. Gustav was woken by Gerhardt at seven with his cup of coffee. Gustav showered and dressed. Gerhardt had selected Gustav's black Hugo Boss business suit, and a freshly ironed shirt with a matching silk tie. Gustav wore his gold cufflinks which had his initials engraved in them. Gustav did not seem nervous about the meeting. But even if he was. He would not let anyone know it. He came down the grand stair case and out onto the terrace for breakfast with the family. Helmut asked him if he was looking forward to the meeting. Gustav said he was.

Heinrich brought the Daimler to the front of the Manor House. He opened the door for Gustav, and He sat in the back of the car. The journey did not take more than ten minutes from the Manor to the municipal offices in the village. The car pulled up and Heinrich opened the door for Gustav to get out. He straightened his tie and ran his hand through his blond hair. In Robert's office on the first floor one of the office juniors was watching out of the window. When he saw Gustav he exclaimed "it's the Kaiser" Robert said "Mr Rothenburg if you do not mind." trying to suppress a chuckle at Gustav's nickname. Soon Gustav had come up the stairs and was in Robert's office. He shook Robert's hand warmly and said hello to the staff. Robert led Gustav to the room where the meeting was being held. The room had tables placed together to make one large table, and expensive leather chairs for the members to sit in. Along the wall was a table set out with flasks of hot water, tea and coffee and biscuits. Robert introduced Gustav to the members of the committee. Gustav thanked them for inviting him. When red

Maggie was introduced to Gustav she refused to shake his hand and told him exactly what she thought of his family and especially him. Gustav did not bat an eye. He just said "Councillor Red Maggie Pettigrew I presume." She looked at him daggers drawn and said "and you must be the Kaiser" the rest of the members quickly ushered everyone into their seats. Gustav was getting warm so he asked if anyone would mind if he took his jacket of. Red Maggie snarled "yes you only want to flash the fact it is a Hugo Boss suit." His well pressed shirt and gold cufflinks did not help either.

Gustav gave his presentation on how the various businesses in the village were working together in the wedding industry to boost tourism in the village and how much the council had saved using the Manor House for seminars, and training courses instead of using the five star hotel in the nearest large town. Red Maggie exclaimed that the council could have done that with the old Manor House if the Heritage organisation had not sold it to the Rothenburgs for a song. Gustav heatedly pointed out that his family had spent a lot of money in restoring a ruin back into a useful building. The meeting broke for tea. Maggie quickly put the knife in. "You have to help yourself here Mr Rothenburg. We don't get waited on here". Gustav said he did not mind. And helped himself. The tension between them continued after the coffee break. She did not like the way Gustav pointed out where in his opinion she was mistaken. She like to remind the meeting of Gustav's privileged upbringing and how he could not possibly understand the problems ordinary people had. Robert did not try to defuse the situation. He rather enjoyed it. The two clashing again and again each one trying to land the knock out blow like two heavyweight boxers. Then Robert had to inform the meeting of a seminar that would be held at the Manor House. The seminar was not residential. But meals would be provided by the Rothenburgs and he thanked them for their hospitality. And members of the committee were invited. Red Maggie winced at the thought of Gustav lording it over them at the Manor. Gustav informed the meeting that the swimming pool would be covered up so that the room could be used for meetings, and that the meals would be served in the ballroom. He said he was looking forward to welcoming them to the Manor and if the weather was fine they could enjoy their refreshments on the terrace. Maggie mocked sarcastically "refreshments on the terrace with cucumber sandwiches." Gustav ignored her and said with Rothenburg reisling of course. The meeting broke for lunch which was a buffet served in another room. Robert, Gustav and the leader of the council sat at one table. Maggie seeing them together said "no wonder you and Mr Rothenburg get on so well Mr Thomas. You both were privately educated were you not" Robert said that he thought she was correct. Gustav snapped "why did you come to Westhampton red Maggie if it is against everything you believe in." She retorted it's not the village it's people like you with your large daimler it's not very green is it." Gustav said "no it's black." he chuckled. "Oh I am so glad that all that money spent on your education was not wasted" she snarled. The afternoon session carried on in the same vein. At the end of the meeting the Chairman thanked Gustav for attending and his useful suggestions. Gustav thanked them once more for his invitation, and then turning to Robert asked "do you want a lift home Robert we all have to do our bit for the environment" Red Maggie went ballistic "you could not care a jot about the environment. So don't try that one on." Gustav sensed now might be a good time to leave. "see you at the next meeting Councillor Pettigrew it has been nice meeting you" Gustav said. She snorted and made no other comment.

THE CHARITY
FOOTBALL MATCH

WESTHAMPTON LIKE ALL other villages had the tensions between the newcomers and the old farming stock like Fred Wright. So the tension was resolved on the field of battle. Well the village football pitch in the annual charity football match to be precise. Fred Wright's young farmers had not lost a match yet. Robert Thomas played and managed the newcomers. On one of his visits to the Manor House. Robert noticed in the family's living room a sport's trophy. He only noticed it because it was one of those inexpensive ubiquitous trophies presented all over the place, and it was so out of character with the family's expensive furniture. But there it was in the display cabinet. So Robert had a closer look at it. It was engraved under thirteen player of the year G L Rothenburg.

Robert exclaimed that Gustav had not told him he could play football. Gustav said modestly that it was some years ago. Robert asked him but you still keep fit don't you. Gustav informed him of his daily swimming exercise to keep in shape. So Robert asked Gustav "would you like to play for the Newcomers Football team this Saturday. Gustav said that he would be delighted.

The match was held on the council owned playing field. It was uneven and muddy. The teams changed in the village Hall. Fred Wright came out of one door with his team. Fred was wearing his tracksuit. Robert came out of another door with his team. And resplendent in his football kit was Gustav. Fred had a last minute talk to his team. If they got the chance nobble the Kaiser. The match began and true to their word they tried to clobber Gustav with fearsome tackles which he avoided much to Fred's annoyance.

The game went on with no one side gaining the upper hand. When the newcomers had a corner. Robert took it. He floated the ball into the goalmouth. Up soared Gustav his head glancing the ball sending it into the top corner of the goal. Then the referee blow the final whistle. Game over Newcomers one young farmers nil goal scored by one G L Rothenburg. Oh the shame for Fred Wright. But worse was to come in the changing rooms Gustav came out of the showers wearing only a towel around his waist. Gustav was not hirsute. In fact he had no hairs on his chest at all.

One of his team mates gave Gustav a bottle of beer, and he placed a still wet arm around Fred Wright and consoled him "you cannot win every game Fred, and it was for a good cause better luck next year". Then it was customary for both teams to go back to the vaults in the Red Lion. Fred Wright's sanctuary from the Kaiser had been breached. He had to endure Gustav's home spun philosophy and his beaming grin. Fred's beer tasted like vinegar. The match did not make Fred and Gustav the best of friends. The sight of Fred's cup in the lounge bar instead of in the vaults did not help. And Robert was only to glad to remind Fred who had scored the winning goal one G L Rothenburg. But for many locals the nickname the Kaiser was a term of endearment. As Gustav and his family had become locals themselves. They felt at home in Westhampton. And especially in the old Manor House. But there were still those for whom the term the Kaiser would be an insult hurled with venom no matter how hard he tried Gustav could not get on with everyone.

GUSTAV'S BIRTHDAY

ROBERT THOMAS CAME into the lounge bar of the Red Lion at noon. He had arranged with Joe the Landlord for him to get him an expensive bottle of a vsop brandy for a birthday present for Gustav. Fred and The Colonel were in the vaults watching the transaction. So they said "oh that looks expensive, who is it for." Robert replied that it was for Gustav it was his birthday present. Fred and the Colonel groaned in unison "Kaiser butt kissing reaches new heights." Robert paid for the bottle and left ignoring their comments. He went to the Old Tea Shoppe for the owner Gloria had made the birthday cake. The surprise party was at half past six that evening. But his parents could not keep a secret from Gustav. So they said it was not until eight.

Robert picked Jane up at the Farmhouse and then drove to the Manor. He looked at his watch it was half past five. They arrived at The Manor House. Gerhardt let them in quietly and they joined the other guests in the ballroom. Around a quarter to six Hildegard said that the servants had not closed all the curtains in the ballroom and would Gustav mind closing them for her. Gustav went and to his surprise the room was in darkness. There was no light coming from the windows. He switched on the lights to make sure that everything was safe. Then hurrah happy birthday they all shouted. The presents were on a table to one side. Robert had bought the bottle of brandy, Jane had given Gustav a pen set with his name engraved on it. The buffet was set out on some tables near by, and on a table by Itself was the cake. Across the room was a banner saying Happy birthday Gustav. Someone in the village was operating the disco. Then at eight the music stopped and the table on which the birthday cake was placed. Was brought into a more prominent position. Hildegard said "Gustav Leopold come and cut your cake." This was soon taken up by all the other guests chanting Gustav Leopold come and cut your cake. Gustav reddened. He cut the first piece and then let Gloria finish the task. Robert announced that they had a collection among Gustav's friends at the Red Lion to buy him a present. It was the custom at the Red Lion for locals to have their own tankard behind the bar. And we thought Gustav should have one too. Robert brought a small box from behind his back, and opened it inside was a tankard. Robert said that they have it engraved. But at the Red Lion

Gustav is not known as Gustav most of the locals refer to him as the Kaiser. So Gustav here is the Kaiser's tankard. Many happy returns.

The party continued until about half past ten. When the guests left to go home. Gustav picked up the brandy bottle and said to his parents, Robert and Jane "come on let's go into the living room for a drink." Robert had hoped he would say that. He was looking forward to sampling the brandy which Joe had recommended. When they had Finished their drinks it was getting late. So Gustav had the servants make up two guest rooms for Robert and Jane. They could stay at the Manor tonight. In the morning they all had breakfast on the terrace. So now the Kaiser was officially twenty five years old.

THE BARN DANCE

St Mark's fund raising committee was having a meeting to discuss their annual Barn Dance. Although it was a way to raise funds in a small village like Westhampton it was one of the social highlights of the year. Gloria said "who knows Gustav might come". Bill Jones a school teacher was also on the fund raising committee. He was a kind man and they all knew that Gloria carried a torch for Gustav. Ever since she had first met him when he came into the shop to ask for directions to the Manor. It was love at first sight for her. Bill knew he had to shatter her illusions "planet earth calling Gloria Gustav lives in the large Manor House, He is waited on by servants, and we all know he does not wash or iron his own clothes. He was privately educated. Gloria people like him would rather be dead than attend our barn dance." Rev Jeremy Browne reluctantly had to agree. Gloria left the meeting her dreams smashed to pieces

As she walked down the high street. She came across Jane Wright, Who noticed at once that Gloria was not her usual over the top happy self. So Jane asked her "what's wrong Gloria". Gloria told Jane all that had happened at the fund raising committee and yes they were right Gustav would never come to the barn dance. Jane was annoyed but not with Gloria. There were people in the village who had made assumptions about Gustav and what he was like. Jane said to Gloria "have you asked Gustav if he is coming to the barn dance you might be surprised" Gloria cheered up. And said "Jane you could not do me a big favour and ask him could you ?". Me and my big mouth thought Jane trapped. "go on then I'll ask him and I will let you know the "answer""

Jane drove to the Manor House for work and parked her mini in her reserved parking Place in front of the Manor. She found Gustav on the terrace finishing his breakfast as usual. He offered her a cup of coffee. Jane picked up her courage and raised the subject of the Barn Dance at the village hall on Friday night and Gloria wants to know if you will be going. Gustav thought for a moment and said "why not back home in Bad Rothenburg we went to all the village dances." Gustav pointed out to Jane that Bad Rothenburg was not a hot bed of social events so the village dances were not to be missed. "I will ask mom it is a while since we have enjoyed a good dance" Gustav said. So not only was Gustav coming but his parents as well.

Jane phoned Gloira and told her the good news that not only was Gustav coming his parents were as well. But she was to keep it a secret. Jane had asked Gustav if he could do the barn dance. He was not sure. Jane knew Gloria she would want to make the dance progressive. That is a certain place in the dance the male partners moved forward so that everyone got to dance with one another. This was Gloria's master plan to ensure that she had one dance with her hero Gustav. So at the Manor in the ballroom Jane and Gustav began intensive training for the big night. Robert on one of his visits to the Manor saw them in the ballroom. "what's this" he said "it's like a scene from the King and I" Gustav swore him to secrecy.

The Village hall was a simple single storey building. It was the hall for the Church St Marks. It was about fifty years old, but the Church was a lot older than that. Inside the hall. The main room was normally where the Sunday school had their lessons, but tonight the chairs were pushed back to form a square. Tables would be at one side for the buffet. Despite it's simple wooden floor tonight it was the annual barn dance. But Bill Jones was right this was not the place you would expect to see Gustav Leopold Rothenburg.

The dance was due to start at half past seven. People began to arrive at seven to get a good seat. Jane had ordered Gloria not to say anything how Gloria managed to keep it secret is a mystery. At a quarter past seven the big black Daimler pulled up outside the Village Hall Heinrich opened the door and first let Helmut, and Hildegard out followed by Gustav. He was dressed casually no black suit or cufflinks, But it was still Hugo Boss. Gustav wore a smart pair of pants and a jacket with a shirt and tie. When the door opened and the Rothenburgs came in you could have heard a pin drop. Well I never the high and mighty Kaiser coming to a village hall barn dance. Everyone stopped chatting and turned and looked at them. But quickly Rev Browne stepped forward shook their hands warmly and took them to their seats.

The barn dance was progressive as Jane had guessed. Gustav and Jane amazed the locals with how well they could dance Fred Astaire and Ginger Rogers watch out. Gloria had her dance with her young blond hero. She was on another planet. Gustav also had a waltz her. In fact the waiting list to dance with Gustav was quite long. Jane's mother who rarely went out wanted to dance with him as well as several members of St Mark's Mothers union. The vicar also danced with Hildegard because he was curious why the family had come it was only a village barn dance. Hildegard laughed when he asked her. She told him that Bad Rothenburg was just like Westhampton not much went on. So the village dances were important social highlights of the year and the family went to everyone. The locals were pleased to see that the family were joining in. Well all but three of them. Red Maggie Pettigrew,

Fred Wright and the Colonel. Gustav noticed them while he was dancing with Jane. So he smiled. Red Maggie said "look at him scheming little German git he is up to something. One of his underhanded tricks" The other two agreed.

The family had donated some cases of Rothenburg wine from Uncle Ernst vineyard. For the night. They stayed at the dance until half past nine when they had arranged to meet Robert in the Red Lion for a nightcap. Red Maggie saw Gustav getting ready to leave. "there he goes for a council of war to Robert Thomas in the pub. I will keep an eye on high and mighty Gustav Rothenburg for a few days" Before the family left the vicar thanked them for coming The ladies from St Marks chatted and said how charming Gustav was. Fred had heard it all before and felt sick. Gustav had a big enough ego without them adding to it with their butt kissing. Gustav turned and waved goodbye "piss off" muttered Red Maggie. Fred and the Colonel laughed.

The family met Robert in the lounge bar of the Red Lion. He had reserved a table for them. Gustav went and ordered the drinks, and when he came with them Robert asked if they had enjoyed the evening. Hildegard was full of it. Robert asked "how was Fred Astaire" Gustav reddened but beamed with delight. Jane said that he passed with flying colours no one suspected a thing. The barn dance was a success for Gloria as she had her dance with her hero Gustav. She talked about it for days afterwards.

THE GRAND SUMMER BALL FOR HILDEGARD'S BIRTHDAY

ON DAY BEFORE leaving for the municipal offices Robert opened his mail. One envelope contained an invitation on embossed paper. Robert Thomas Esq is cordially invited to a grand summer ball to be held in the Old Manor House on the occasion of Hildegard Rothenburg's birthday, and underneath Gustav had written a ps we will have a drink at the Red Lion first. It was a formal black tie event so both men were at the Red Lion in their evening suits Gustav as always on occasions like these wore his gold cufflinks which were engraved with his initials. As they came out of the Red Lion Red Maggie and her friends saw them. Red Maggie said "look we must be near the Zoo there are the penguins". much to the amusement of her friends. She continued "my invitation must have got lost in the post" Gustav in Germanic directness simply said you were not invited. "Good" maggie retorted "I would not have wanted to come anyway" "Oh and Gustav don't choke on your Canapés and champagne while thinking of the poor in Westhampton". Gustav ignored her comments and entered the Daimler. Maggie made some unlady like comments which thankfully Robert and Gustav could not here as the car drove away.

They stopped at Wright's farmhouse to pick up Jane. She had bought an expensive evening dress for the occasion. Her father thought she was mixing with an odd crowd.

The Daimler pulled up outside the Manor House near to the grand front door. They rang the bell and Gerhardt let them in. The grand ball was being held in the ballroom with refreshments and drinks served in the drawing room. Next door. There was a banner across the ballroom wishing Hildegard a happy birthday. The ballroom looked impressive with it's elaborate ceilings and gilt chandeliers. The dark blue velvet curtains were drawn back. So that people could go out onto the terrace which was decorated with fairy lights. It was a warm summer's evening.

Some local musicians formed a string quartet. They were playing Strauss waltzes Robert, Gustav, and Jane were chatting together. When Gloria approached them. Jane noticed her coming and said "Gustav here comes the statue of liberty" knowing Gloria carried a torch for Gustav and was besotted with him. Gloria hoped that Gustav would ask her to dance with him, and being a gentleman Gustav did not disappoint her. They had a waltz in the ballroom. She was on cloud nine dancing with her heart throb. Jane looked at Robert and said "we ought to let her know that he's gay and she is wasting her time" Robert said "no let's not spoil the night for her she will find out soon enough" Gustav danced with Jane. Then the three of them went out onto the terrace with their drinks. Sparkling wine from Uncle Ernst of course.

Later on Robert and Gustav were talking with some of the parish councillors, who Gustav got on with. Robert joked "Red Maggie Pettigrew's at the door wanting to come in" Gustav responded with words that should not be repeated and the others laughed. Gloria had made the birthday cake which was on a occasional table. They brought the table into the centre of the ballroom and invited her to cut the cake., which was followed by them singing happy birthday. The buffet had been made by Joe from the Red Lion. The village all pulled together on occasions like these. The ballroom resembled a film set with it's elaborate ceilings, gilt chandeliers, and the strauss music. Robert guided Gustav onto to the terrace. "Do your parents know about us" he asked. Gustav said that his parents knew he was gay and that he would properly adopt some children to keep the family line going. Both his parents knew Robert was his lover and approved of his choice. Jane came out of the ballroom and said "come on you two lovebirds there's a party going on in here and you will be missed.

When most of the other guest had gone home. The family and their small intimate circle of friends withdrew into the family's living room. The men had whisky and Hildegard and Jane cocktails well it was Hildegard's birthday. Hildegard looked at Robert and said "come on when are you going to make a honest man out of my son" Gustav blushed. Robert replied that he and Gustav had talked about it, but that they had made no serious decisions yet. Hildegard said that she thought that they were a perfect couple made for each other. Then laughing she said "by the way Robert you do know that he likes to get his own way" Robert said that he was well aware of that. Helmut stood up and placed a hand of Robert's shoulder and became serious "take care of Gustav" Gustav told them to stop it or he would end up crying like a baby. Hildegard laughed "well that's nothing new is it"

It was late so the family invited Robert and Jane to stay the night at the manor, and in the morning they all had breakfast on the terrace. It was a lovely summer's day the gardens were well cared for and the stream ran in the distance. Robert thought it was great to be alive and was relieved that their secret was now out in the open.

THE SKELETON IN
THE WARDROBE

ROBERT SHOULD HAVE guessed that a family as old as the
Rothenburgs had their fair share of black sheep. But it all
came out one evening as the family and friends were having
a relaxing drink in their private quarters. The council was
planning a careers day for the children. Naturally Robert
thought that Gustav would be ideal with his business
experience. So in the conversation he raised the topic and
asked Gustav if he would like to come along. And explain
why he entered the wine business. Gustav was always keen
to support the council's events, But this time Gustav said
he did not know if he was available, and moved about
in his armchair as though it was uncomfortable. Then
Hildegard spoke "Robert what Gustav is trying to say
and making a right mess of it. Is the Rothenburg family
started their wine business in 1761 and since then every

Rothenburg with the exception of one man who opted for the priesthood and whose name is never mentioned again in family conversations have worked for the family business. The option of not working for the family business does not exist for a Rothenburg. Gustav was told at a early age where his future lie. He was a Rothenburg and he would work for the family business. And no son of mine was going to bring shame on my part of the family by not entering the family business." Robert saw Gustav wince. Hildegard continued "the only choice that Gustav had was the role he would play in the business with his natural aptitude for figures he was trained as an accountant" "it may seem old fashioned to people outside the family. But that is how we are. And Gustav's children when he has them will learn they too have to work in the family business". So Robert by accident had touched a nerve the one subject that was taboo in Rothenburg circles of not working for the family. Robert and Jane could not believe it, but Hildegard was deadly serious about the issue.

Gustav could talk about the family business and his experience, but what if a child asked him why he had entered into it. It seemed old fashioned. Gustav could lie but he did not want to. Robert's parents had sent him to university in order to get a good career and it was his choice to enter local government. Jane had never thought of Gustav as being a member of a strict society like the mafia, but the Rothenburgs had their code of obedience to the family business and Gustav had to honour it.

Robert saw Gustav in a whole new light Robert's surname was Thomas and that was that. But Gustav was a Rothrenburg and there seemed to be a lot of baggage attached to that. All around the Manor the Rothenburg coat of arms was displayed a constant reminder to Gustav of his responsibilities. The conversation soon changed and Hildegard became her normal cheerful self once more. But Robert never forgot about the skeleton in the Rothenburg wardrobe. The one member of the family who had opted for the priesthood instead of his ascribed role in the family business and whose name was never mentioned again.

Robert thought that Gustav had a privileged lifestyle, but now he knew that there was a price to pay for it. Gustav had to accept his role in the family business whatsoever Gustav would have been good at would have been his role in the firm. He could not do as he wished. The locals mocked Gustav for hius lavish lifestyle and sometimes Robert wanted to explain to them the true cost for Gustav. But they would not believe someone was forced to follow the family trade anymore.

Then Robert looked at Gustav. Thankfully for him life in the family business was no real hardship for him. He loved the peace and quiet of the Manor His walks around the grounds and breakfast on the terrace. Robert could not see Gustav in a normal working environment. Gustav was well suited to being woken up at seven by Gerhardt with his cup of coffee Opening the curtains while Gustav came to in his four poster bed in his silk pyjamas. Robert knew that Gustav liked being a Rothenburg. Gustav was a snob and enjoyed it.

Because it was a lovely summer's evening. They brought their drinks out onto the terrace. This was Gustav's world. He belonged here and as they chatted together it was as though the delicate topic had not been raised The villagers might think of Gustav as a rebel, but he would not bring shame on his mother's side of the family. Not when it came to the family business. Gustav was and always would be a Rothenburg.

THE COFFEE MORNING

GLORIA WAS ON her way to open the Old Tea Shoppe when she came across Jane Wright coming out of the village store. Gloria is a lovely person but if she stopped you in the street it could be a while before you politely managed to get away. Jane was trapped and soon Gloria brought the conversation around to her favourite subject Gustav. Jane could understand why Gloria carried a torch for him. He was very good looking. He was five foot eleven inches tall and about twelve stones in weight but some of the ladies wanted to fatten him up. But as Robert Thomas said you cannot fatten a thoroughbred.

St Marks were having a Coffee morning on Saturday for some overseas charity and would Gustav be able to come. The ladies of the w I would be so pleased if Gustav could come. Jane asked her what time it started. Gloria told her at ten o'clock. Jane stressed that Gustav was very busy.

Gloria looked depressed. But Jane knew Gustav's Achilles heel. "will there be any cream cakes on sale" Jane asked. "why yes" said Gloria "in fact Mrs Smith at number 47 has just started making Black Forest gateaus in honour of the Rothenburgs and I believe they are very good" Jane asked "with cream" Gloria finally understood what Jane was saying "yes with all the cream Gustav wants" Jane said "I think I can persuade him to come"

Jane arrived at the Manor House Gustav had finished his breakfast and was walking in the garden. Jane stopped in her tracks Gustav was wearing jeans. Jane thought that they were properly expensive ones. But Gustav in jeans it wasn't his public image. Jane brought up the subject of the coffee morning at St Mark's Church Hall on Saturday morning and Gloria wondered if he would be able to come. Then Jane played her trump card "oh and by the way there is at woman in the W I who has started making Black Forest Cherry cakes with Cream and they are to die for She will have some there on Saturday morning." Caught hook line and sinker Jane one Gustav nil. Jane said "I could even pick you up in my mini" Gustav thought about it for a moment visualizing himself getting out of a mini. It just wasn't Gustav Rothenburg. "No thank you I Will pick you up in the Daimler at the farmhouse on Saturday. He said. Jane said "thanks" and then she realised just what Gustav had said that he would pick her up at the farmhouse on Saturday morning. Her father would either have the twelve bore shotgun ready or the muck spreader to bury Gustav in horse manure when he finds out.

Jane was having tea in the farmhouse when she dropped her bombshell "oh by the way Gustav's coming to pick me up on Saturday morning there's a coffee morning at St Mark's Church Hall". "that's nice" remarked her mother. Then the penny dropped with Fred. "The Kaiser's coming here that blond streak of piss coming into my house no way. He can pick you up at the door, but I'm not having him in my house not over my dead body I have to endure listening to his voice in the Red Lion but there is no way he is coming into my house" Fred was fuming. "Why not dear the women in the mothers union say that he is a lovely young man" Jane's mother said. Fred said to Jane "See he's even spreading his influence in my own home".

Saturday morning came and Gustav would pick Jane up at Wright's Farmhouse at nine forty in the morning. The big black Daimler pulled into Wright's farmyard and Heinrich got out to open the car door for Gustav. Gustav knocked on the farmhouse door. Jane's mother was determined to meet Gustav. So she hurried to answer the door. She opened the door and chatted to Gustav for about five minutes. Fred was having his breakfast and he could hear Gustav at the front door. "oh if only I had the muck spreader ready he would be up to his neck in good old horse muck" Fred groaned. Jane took the hint and spirited Gustav away. Jane's mother closed the door after them and said" what a lovely young man why don't you like him dear?" Fred just sat there at the table with his head in his hands.

The Daimler pulled up outside St Mark's Church Hall Heinrich opened the door for them to get out. Gustav and Jane entered the Church Hall. Gloria was onto Gustav straight away "oh what a surprise Gustav you've come" Jane thought you lying beggar I told you yesterday that he was coming. Rev Jeremy Browne Managed to free Gustav from Gloria and she went back behind her stall. Gustav was wearing a cashmere sweater and jeans well they were Hugo Boss jeans. In front of them was Mrs Smith's cake stall. And in the middle was the Black Forest cherry cake already cut in slices. Gustav found a reason to head towards her stall. Mrs Smith had been forwarned so she was one step ahead of Gustav she had a plate ready with a piece on it with some Cream as well. How he managed to remain twelve stones is a mystery. Gustav sat at a table and devoured the cake with great delight. Then he and Jane had a look at the various stalls. He bought some raffle tickets and saw the items for sale on the crafts stall to which he politely said no thank you. They sat down at a table to have their coffees. Thankfully Gloria was kept busy behind her stall to bother Gustav. But the other elderly ladies from the W I came over to chat with Gustav, and a woman who had her white westie with her managed to get Gustav to hold her beloved dog on his knee while she had her coffee. Jane wished that she had her camera with her. Gustav in jeans with a westie on his knee priceless. About half past eleven Gustav and Jane left the Coffee morning. Gustav stopped outside to brush the dog hairs off his jeans, and Jane came behind carrying a box with a Black Forest Cherry cake in it. He insisted that it was for his mother. Jane said that she would ask Hildegard on Monday.

JANE'S BIRTHDAY AT THE RED LION

Jane thought that it would be easier to have her birthday party at the Red Lion than at the Farmhouse. Besides Joe the landlord served a excellent buffet and it was reasonable priced too. So Jane contacted Joe and arranged the evening.

At tea Jane informed her Father and Mother that she had booked the Lounge bar at the Red Lion for her birthday party. It was Fred's local so he was pleased and her Mother rarely went out socially so for her this would be a treat. Then Fred saw the fly in the ointment "you've invited the Kaiser haven't you" Jane protested "well I do work for him and he is really nice when you get to know him it's only for a couple of hours you can be nice to him for a least that long." Fred groaned "oh alright then for a couple of hours but he has not got to wear his black suit or those flashy cufflinks" and Jane demanded "and you must call him Gustav not the

Kaiser" Fred agreed for a couple of hours he would pretend
to like Gustav well be civil to him at least. He knew that his
drinking partner Colonel Price-Waters would be laughing
at the spectacle from the other bar. Jane said that she would
inform Gustav that it was an informal casual affair so no
black suit or cufflinks. Jane's Mother had only met Gustav
once, but she liked him and was looking forward to seeing
him again.

On the evening of the party the Wrights were already
in the lounge bar of the Red Lion. Joe had hung a banner
across the room wishing Jane a happy birthday. At one side
of the room two tables had been pushed together and the
buffet was laid out on them. At seven o'clock the door to the
lounge bar opened and in came Robert and Gustav, who was
wearing a Ralph Lauren polo shirt and some well tailored
pants. Even casual Gustav looked smart. But you could not
miss the expensive gold rolex wristwatch on his wrist. Fred
groaned "it's here" Jane mouthed be nice. Her mother came
over and kissed Gustav. So too did Gloria who as usual had
made the birthday cake. Robert and Gustav selected what
they wanted to eat from the buffet and then ordered their
drinks and sat down. Gustav and his parents had given Jane
a bottle of champagne \ and it was with her other presents
on a small table.

During the evening Robert and Gustav went to the
toilets. Robert saw that the toilets were empty and pushed

Gustav into one of the cubicles and said "I cannot wait to tear the clothes of you" to Gustav. Gustav replied "patience Robert everything comes to him who waits" Robert pulled Gustav close to him and kissed him and ruffled his hair. They went back outside and Jane noticed that Gustav's hair had been ruffled.

I should have said and no hanky panky between Robert and Gustav tonight as well Jane thought. Gloria Brown was still hoping to catch Gustav's heart. It had not taken Jane long to work out that Gustav was gay and Robert was his lover. Jane smiled to herself she never consider herself a fag hag before.

Everyone did there party pieces. Gustav recited some verses in English of the Lorley rock poem he had learned as a child in Bad Rothenburg. Robert could recite monologues like Sam pick up your musket. And Fred when he had a few pints sang a few folk songs.

At ten o'clock the party began to wind down. Heinrich appeared at the lounge door to take Gustav and Robert home. Gustav waved goodbye to the party. Jane thought no sleep for you two tonight. The Colonel came from the other bar into the lounge bar and asked Fred "well did you manage to be civil to the Kaiser for a couple of hours then" Jane glowed at him and said "Gustav! His name is Gustav". "yes and he is a lovely young man" added Jane's mother. "See what I Have to put up with" Fred moaned "two of them in his fan club". Then Fred told the colonel that tonight he had not been that bad. Gustav had not worn his black business suit or wore his gold cufflinks. But he still had his airs and graces. Jane defended Gustav saying that he could not help that he was brought up that way. Joe the landlord thought the night had gone well. Fred and Gustav had not been at each others throats. Fred would never be Gustav's friend but at least tonight he was civil to Gustav. Jane was pleased that she had taken the risk of inviting both of them to her party. And demanding that her father tried to get on with Gustav. But it was soon over Fred and the Colonel were referring to him as the Kaiser even before they had left the pub. Jane and her Mother just looked at each other it was a battle that they were never going to win. Jane said "come on let's go home and open that bottle of champagne Gustav gave me" Fred said "vot a gut idea Jane" mocking Gustav's accent. Jane said "don't be so cruel" then bust out laughing it was so like Gustav

GUSTAV'S SETBACKS

GUSTAV DID NOT have everything his own way in the village, which for someone like Gustav was irksome to say the least. But there were two notable defeats for him.

The first one was when he wanted to make his parents feel more at Home in Westhampton. He wanted to rename the Manor House Schloss Rothenburg or Castle Rothenburg. And He asked Robert how he should raise the matter with the council. Robert and some of Gustav's other candid friends told him it was not a good idea and that it would not be well received in the village. Robert thought especially the vaults of the Red Lion. When Fred heard he was almost speechless all he could keep saying was Schloss Rothenburg.

Well English Heritage did not like the idea of an eighteenth century English Manor House being called Schloss Rothenburg. So the idea died a death.

Gustav next idea caused more trouble. There was a bridle path which went along side the Manor House and from the bridle path people could see the family out on the terrace. So Gustav's solution was that access to the bridle path should be reduced. The matter was to be resolved in a public meeting to be held in the village hall. Red Maggie Pettigrew had been circulating leaflets against the idea, and Fred Wright had an idea to ruffle the Kaiser's feathers. He knew that wherever Gustav went he expected people to stand out of the way and was annoyed if they did not. So Fred had organised a picket of young farmers to block Gustav's way into the meeting.

The evening of the meeting came and the hall was packed. The meeting started at seven o'clock. Gustav and Robert arrived in the Daimler around half past six. The Chauffeur opened the door for them to get out. Gustav was wearing his Hugo Boss business suit but he was trying to look casual he was not wearing a tie and had his shirt top button undone. Gustav approached the entrance to the village hall and the young farmers stood their ground. They would not get out of the way for Gustav. The local village bobby saw what was going on and called on them to allow Mr Rothenburg through. As Gustav passed them they jostled him against the door post. Robert went to help Gustav and asked him if he was hurt. He was not he was just annoyed. Fred had ruffled the Kaiser's feathers.

Gustav came into the hall running his hand through his hair.

There was a table at the front of the meeting at which sat Gustav, Robert, and the leader of the council. Gustav outlined his proposal to a quiet room. Red Maggie spoke against it. Robert tried a compromise by showing on a map how the bridle path might make a slight detour away from the Manor. But Gustav's enemies did not want him to have a partial victory so they opposed that as well. The vicar and Gloria spoke up for Gustav. But they were shouted down. The Colonel could see that Gustav was getting impatient He was running his hand through his hair and looking at his wristwatch. So the Colonel chided him "What's the matter Gustav are your puppets not dancing to your tune tonight?. The audience laughed. Then Fred Wright stood up and said "ever since the Kaiser had come to the village he has been trying to get his own way. Well high and mighty Gustav Rothenburg your are not getting your way over this." and sat down to great applause. When it was put to the vote it was soundly defeated. The trio of Gustav's enemies taunted him as he sat there stony faced.

After the meeting Gustav, Robert and some of the Councillors were chatting together. When Red Maggie said "well the Kaiser party took a good kicking tonight" Gustav glowed at her. Robert suggested to Gustav that they go to the Red Lion for a drink. But Gustav declined he was not in a good mood. Then Heinrich appeared at the front door Gustav walked towards him, and Fred and the rest of the gang taunted him "Heinrich nach Hause all the way home to Bad Rothenburg" Gustav was livid and was going to say something, but he decided against it and sat back in the Daimler trying to appear relaxed. The battle of wills between Gustav and Red Maggie were not over.

Gustav would go away and lick his wounds and come back fighting. Robert knew that Gustav would sulk for a while, but by tomorrow he would be his own self again. Robert also knew that his parents would not stand for Gustav acting like a diva.

THE CRICKET MATCH

It was not all work in the village. One Saturday there was to be a cricket match between Westhampton and the nearby village. Robert asked Gustav and his parents if they had ever been to a cricket match. Gustav had heard about cricket but was not sure of all the rules. So Robert invited them to come along. He pointed out that the match normally lasted all day and that people brought a picnic and there would be a beer tent.

So on the Saturday morning Robert arrived early and selected a good spot for a picnic. The big black Daimler pulled up and the family got out of the car. Heinrich opened the boot and they took out some chairs, and a blanket and a large picnic hamper. The Rothenburgs did not do picnics by half. The hamper was full of good food and wine.

It was a beautiful sunny day Hildegard had a large sun hat Gustav wore a white Ralph Lauren polo shirt and white flannels. Fred and the Colonel saw him and asked him if he had come to see the Westhampton rain dance Gustav was bemused. Fred put an arm around Gustav and Said that two pieces of wood were set twenty two yards apart not an inch more or less Two men came out in traditional village garb and eleven other men in white made a circle around them. Then one of the villagers around them rubbed a ball on his trousers and ran towards them and it starts to rain. Fred and the Colonel both burst out laughing. Gustav realised that they were pulling his leg again. So he stormed off saying "verruckt" crazy or mad.

The vicar was there with the Bishop, who had come on his annual visit to the parish. The Bishop's visits always made Rev Browne nervous. He spotted the Rothenburgs and their picnic and brought the Bishop to them. Rev Browne took great pride in telling the Bishop that they were part of the flock at St Mark's. In fact they were the new owners of the restored Manor. Hildegard invited the Bishop to join them. Gustav gave the Bishop his chair. Hildegard was interested in his stories. Soon it was obvious the Bishop had forgotten about Rev Browne So Gustav and Robert took him to the beer tent. The vicar said he would go with them but only have a half pint. Robert ordered some of the cask ale Joe had brought. Robert and Gustav had pints. The vicar said how the Bishop had arrived that morning, but always moaned about the vicarage. Gustav noticed how well the Bishop and his mother were getting on. S o Gustav asked the vicar "do you mind if we ask the Bishop if he would like to stay at the Manor" Rev Browne was delighted the Bishop could come with the family on Sunday morning in the Daimler. So Gustav phoned the Manor and had a guest room made up.

They went back to the party and Gustav asked his mother if the Bishop would like to stay with them. Hildegard thought it was a splendid idea. So too did the Bishop when he heard that he would now be staying in an eighteenth century Manor House in a four poster bed. Gustav said that he had already made arrangements for the Bishop. Hildegard and the Bishop hardly noticed the game both were enjoying the picnic and the wine. Robert tried to explain the finer points of the game to Helmut and Gustav. But the idea of a game lasting all day with no one winning seemed strange but they made two trips to the beer tent. Gustav would nod as though he understood what Robert was saying about the match. When in fact he had not a clue.

About five o'clock Heinrich came back with the Daimler. They packed all the items in the boot and the Bishop sat back into the Daimler's cream leather seats. As they came near the Manor. The Bishop saw it's imposing front door. The servants took his luggage up to his bedroom while the family went onto the terrace for tea. Hildegard showed the Bishop around the grounds. They had the evening meal in the drawing room and then withdrew into the family's private quarters for brandies. Hildegard had her sweet sherry. Hildegard loved listening to the Bishop's anecdotes. The Bishop retired to his room about ten o'clock. In the morning Gerhardt woke him with a cup of tea at half past seven. They all had breakfast together on the terrace. Then they travelled to St Mark's in the Daimler. The Bishop had a soft spot for the comfort of the Daimler and the Manor House. The Bishop preached the sermon and he thanked the parish for it's hospitality especially the Rothenburgs. And how he hoped to visit the parish more often. Rev Browne was not impressed with that news. After the service the congregation shook the Bishop's hand. He thanked Hildegard for her hospitality She said she was delighted and whenever he came to Westhampton he would have to stay at the Manor House which was just what the Bishop hoped she would say. Gustav gave him a bottle of Rothenburg wine as a gift. Then they took the Bishop to the station in the Daimler. Heinrich carried the Bishop's luggage to the train

The Bishop sat back in his seat. He had enjoyed the whole weekend away in Westhampton Parish The Cricket match and the picnic with the Rothenburgs. He had appreciated the hospitality of the flock at St Mark's especially the Manor House. The Four poster bed, refreshments on the terrace. And Hildegard listening to his tales the walk along the river in the grounds of the Manor had given him some new thoughts for his sermon. Westhampton parish was a place he would be visiting more often now. Even if Rev Jeremy Browne did not approve. The Bishop chuckled.

THE VILLAGE FAIR

WESTHAMPTON HAD ITS annual village fair. When all the village came and enjoyed itself. The Womens Institute had a stall selling home made chutneys, cakes, and Jams. The Red Lion would have a beer tent. There would be Morris dancing, and fancy dress. The village green would be decorated with bunting. This would be the Rothenburgs first village fair. In the Red Lion Fred and The Colonel were hatching a plan. There was a game for charity where someone would be placed in the pillory and have wet sponges thrown at them. It was meant to be a bit of fun and all for a good cause. But they were planning to get Gustav in the pillory and let out their venom against him with wet sponges. Joe the landlord overheard their plotting, and said Gustav's a decent lad He has put plenty of business my way, and given me a good discount on the wines He has sold me. Why cannot you leave him alone ?. Fred was silent for a moment. Then said

"Joe you have not joined his fan club as well have you ?"
Joe did not reply but he was determined to warn Gustav of
their plan. He warned Robert Thomas. So that Gustav was
on his guard at the fair.

So a team was set up consisting of Robert, Jane, Gloria
and Joe to thwart Fred and the Colonel's plan. The day
of the fair was a bright summer's day. Helmut, Hildegard
and Gustav arrived in the black Daimler. They went first
to the Womens Institute stall to purchase some homemade
chutneys and Jams. Robert took them to the beer tent so
that they could sample some of the cask ales. Fred and the
Colonel were trying to catch Gustav on his own, but the
team never left him alone. As they finished their drinks in
the beer tent. Gustav looked at his watch and said "Robert
it is time I went to the Pillory. I know what all my trusted
friends have been doing trying to protect me. But I will
not melt and it might be fun. I know the locals see me as
being remote and aloof, and Fred and the Colonel want to
catch me in their trap. Let's spring it for them. So the party
headed towards the pillory. Joe the landlord from the Red
Lion was running it and He did not want to let Gustav have
a go. Gustav assured him not to worry everything would be
alright. Gustav took off his shirt and handed it to Robert
saying "look after this Robert I do not want to get it wet".
Fred and the Colonel were delighted they thought they had
won. But then they heard some of the local women saying

"cor look at him He's as fit as a butcher's dog" Gustav was in the pillory for around ten minutes. Fred and the Colonel and others threw wet sponges at Gustav and He got soaked., but it was fun. Gustav was not hirsute. He did not have a manly hairy chest. But he did have a firm six pack. Gustav was given a towel by Joe and He asked for a comb for his hair. Gustav was always a dandy. Robert handed him back his shirt. Robert told Gustav that there had been cries of get them off meaning his clothes. Gustav teased Robert "From you Robert" Robert laughed and said he had thought about it. Fred and his mates were in the beer tent drowning their sorrows. Fred said "so much for our grand plan. The kraut ruined it." The colonel remarked that the Germans have always been keen on physical education. But the Kaiser flashing his body to the village. Fred was speechless "those darn women fancying the Kaiser. I cannot believe it". Joe behind the bar was quietly smiling to himself they had spiked their guns. Gustav had not been made a fool of. And He had won some new friends. People who now realised that He was not the stuff shirt they presumed he was. He did have a sense of humour. Robert knew that when Gustav took off his shirt. He would impress the ladies. But they could look but not touch that delight was only for him.

To make things worse for Fred and the Colonel. Robert, Helmut, Hildegard, Jane and Gustav came into the beer tent. Robert ordered the drinks. Hildegard was elated saying" people think Gustav has been spoilt but today we showed them we can have a laugh as well as anyone." Jane said that Gustav could have been a male model. Robert said don't give him any ideas. So after celebrating their success the family went home in the Daimler. Fred was livid the Kaiser had upstaged them. He had turned their foolproof plan against him into one of boosting his image in the village. But the one thing Fred could not understand. The women ogling the Kaiser. That blond streak of piss whatever next.

WESTHAMPTON COTTAGE HOSPITAL

ROBERT REMEMBERS THE events clearly. It all started one day in the Red Lion pub. Where Robert and Gustav were having their weekly drink together. When Gustav complained of a pain in the right hand side of his abdomen. Robert knew it must be something serious as Gustav never complained about anything. So Robert urged his friend to go and see his Doctor as soon as possible. Gustav assured Robert that he would.

A few days later Gustav was in a meeting of the tourism committee in the Municipal offices. They were in the committee room having a tea break. When Gustav doubled up in pain and fell to the floor. Robert guessed that Gustav had not taken his advice and gone and seen his doctor. The Councillors were worried their important guest was seriously ill. They had a first aid person from the building come and examine Gustav who was holding his abdomen and looked pale. The first aid assistant told Robert that he would have to call an ambulance. When the ambulance arrived the paramedic examined Gustav and said that Gustav would have to go to the Westhampton Cottage Hospital as soon as possible.

The ambulance took Gustav to the Hospital. Robert followed the Daimler back to the Manor House to inform Gustav's parents what had happened. They gathered Gustav's pyjamas slippers and dressing gown. Gerhardt collected Gustav's shaving kit and toilet bag. Then Robert showed Heinrich the way to the hospital. In the Daimler were Helmut and Hildegard. Along with Robert was Jane Wright.

When they arrived at the Hospital. They found Gustav on a trolley in a cubicle. His mother by now was almost in tears Hildegard ran her hand through his hair and kissed him on the cheek. And said "my baby's not well" Deep down the tough matriarch spoiled Gustav.

A Doctor came into the cubicle opened Gustav's shirt and lowered his trousers to examine his abdomen. "Does this hurt Mr Rothenburg" Gustav just managed to keep on the trolley. He winced and said "yes". The doctor simply said "em I would suggest that you have a inflamation of the vermiform appendix" Gustav looked at him none the wiser. "appendicitis it will have to come out". Gustav signed a consent form and a male nurse shaved him lower down his abdomen in preparation for the operation. He was weighed and had his blood group determined. Then Gustav was taken to the theatre by now his mother was crying and Jane not far off. Gustav was in the theatre for one and a half to two hours. When he came out a nurse was making sure he was alright. Gustav was mumbling incoherently. He was still out for the count. Gustav along with his pyjamas and slippers went to one of the wards. Robert thought this was going to be fun the Kaiser in a hospital ward.

Ward one six o'clock in the morning. The curtains were drawn back in the ward and a nurse came up to Gustav's bed, and woke a sleepy Gustav. "Good morning Mr Rothenburg how are you feeling this morning". He replied "Gustav call me Gustav and I'm sore". She kindly told him that was to be expected for a few days. And then had him change from the hospital gown into his own silk pyjamas. While he was changing into them he noticed the dressing lower down his abdomen. Then he went to the bathroom to shave and freshen up. Then the patients had breakfast at a table one of the other patients recognised Gustav. "cor blimey it's the Kaiser" he said. But Gustav was too ill to respond. After breakfast it was the Doctor's round. He looked at the dressing and said "how do you feel Mr Rothenburg" Gustav said "call me Gustav and I'm sore". The Doctor did not show a wonderful bedside manner. He just said that was to be expected and moved on to the next patient. Gustav would have to stay in hospital for a couple of days at least.

At visiting time Hildegard, Jane and Helmut arrived. Poor Helmut he was the beast of burden carrying the bunches of flowers. His mother and Jane made a fuss of Gustav. Fred back home at the farmhouse had asked his daughter Jane if the shop sold drop dead cards as well. Jane promptly burst into tears and said how could he be so cruel. Even in his own home Fred could not enjoy the thought of the Kaiser being in agony in the council offices. Jane knew that Gustav was not well he did not complain about the food or the bed. But after a few days Gustav said that the food was not fit to be served to pigs, and the bed was too small for him to get a proper nights sleep. The old Gustav was back well minus his appendix. They borrowed a wheelchair to take him to the entrance of the hospital. Gustav told them not to make such a fuss he could walk. But the doctors had insisted that he take it easy for a while. After a few days a nurse came to the Manor to remove the stitches and make sure that Gustav was healing. He would have a small scar even when he was swimming you could still see the scar above his speedos. When Robert called on Gustav. He was shown the scar. When Gloria heard Gustav was out of the hospital she was delighted. She had made him a cake to welcome him home. Soon he was back in the lounge bar at the Red Lion. They all welcomed him back. Well except Fred and the Colonel.

Fred said "I would have kept the appendix and thrown him away." The Colonel said don't ask about the operation for he will show you the scar. You would have thought he had been awarded the purple heart the way he goes on.

It was true over the next few weeks Gustav told anyone who would listen about his near death experience. Robert thought serious certainly, But near death was a slight exaggeration. Then Robert recalled the scene in the hospital before Gustav was wheeled down to the theatre. His mother in tears saying her baby was not well and he too had held Gustav's hand and told his dear friend that everything would be alright.

HALLOWEEN IN
WESTHAMPTON

JOE THE LANDLORD at the Red Lion Pub had seen the children in the village preparing for halloween and that was when he had the idea. Why should the children have all the fun. He decided that the Red Lion should have a Halloween party for adults. So Joe had the posters displayed around the village.

Jane saw one of the posters and thought it would be a good night out. Westhampton was a quiet village where not much happened. The village needed a party. Jane arrived for work at the Manor House Gustav was finishing his breakfast in the drawing room and he offered Jane a cup of coffee before they started work. So Jane asked Gustav if he wanted to come to the Halloween party fancy dress was optional. Jane stressed that it would be a laugh and Joe was serving Hot pot and Red Cabbage with Apple pie and Cream. Jane had to explain to Gustav exactly what Hot Pot was He knew that Red cabbage was similar to sour kraut. Jane said she knew of a shop in the nearest large town where they could obtain fancy dress costumes for the night. After much persuasion Gustav agreed to go. As did Helmut and Hildegard but they decided against going in fancy dress.

Gustav opted for a Dracula outfit, Jane decided on a Witch's costume with a long black wig and a Witch's hat. Robert picked a zombie outfit. On the night they met at the Manor. Jane applied some make up on Gustsv's face to make him look paler. Robert had make up on to resemble a zombie. At seven they all entered the Daimler and headed for the Red Lion. The party was being held in the lounge bar. Joe had decorated it with plastic spider's webs, pumpkins, and skeletons.

About a quarter past seven the Daimler arrived at the Red Lion. Heinrich opened the door for Helmut, Hildegard and then Gustav followed by Robert and Jane. Gustav's cape was flowing in the night air. They all entered the lounge bar. Red Maggie saw Gustav coming in as Dracula, and she said "so he's come as a blood sucking vampire. What else would you expect from parasites like the Rothenburgs." Fred and the Colonel laughed.

Joe had added food colouring to the drinks to make them look horrible. When they tasted quite nice. Gustav chatted to the other guests his face had white make up on and he wore bright red lip stick and fangs. Robert had gruesome scars on his face in make up. The lounge bar was full of zombies, vampires and Witches. With ghosts and other monsters. The Rothenburgs had never tasted Hot Pot before but they enjoyed it. Gloria had made some of her cakes which were decorated with blood red or black food colouring.

Red Maggie Pettigrew wished that she had a stake for a certain vampire. She wished that the theme for fancy dress had been the French revolution and Gustav had been a aristocrat. She would have loved to have been operating the Guillotine for Gustav. "I would have chopped his head off for nothing. It would have been a pleasure". She said. The others at her table laughed she disliked the Rothenburgs in general. But with Gustav the hatred was personal

Gustav could be seen clearly with his blond hair in the throng of the other guests. Robert, Jane and Gustav were enjoying the fancy dress. There were traditional village games like apple bobbing. Gustav had to kneel over a large bowl with his hands behind his back and try to take an apple from the water with his mouth. They all laughed as Gustav failed. Robert tried to pick up an apple as well without success.

Gloria chatted to Gustav. Fred called Gustav by his forename of Gustav instead of calling him the Kaiser. Jane was speechless it was not like her father. Even Red Maggie said good evening Mr Rothenburg well she would never call him Gustav. Hildegard was asking Joe the recipe for the Hot Pot. Gustav looked at Robert and knew that He would be having Hot Pot for evening meal in a couple of days. Gustav had a sweet tooth so he enjoyed the apple pie and cream.

Joe asked Gustav to select the winner of the fancy dress. Gustav was delighted to be the Judge because he did not want to win it anyhow. He decided on another zombie who had a knife through his head. The decision was a popular one. Helmut had chosen some dark red wine for Joe for tonight from the Rothenburg selection. It went well with the theme. Helmut being a true Rothenburg with wine in his blood made sure that the wine was of the best quality.

The party carried on until around ten o'clock. Heinrich opened the door of the Red Lion and indicated to the family that he was ready to take them home. Gustav spread his cape and pretended he was floating down the stairs of the pub like Dracula. Joe saw them off and thanked them for coming. The first Halloween party in Westhampton at the Red Lion had been a resounding success. The wine Joe had sold to the customers was from Uncle Ernst vineyard in Bad Rothenburg. Which Gustav had sold to Joe at a discount. So the family had made some money out of the party as well. Gustav ever the accountant was always seeking new ways to extend the family business. Gustav was right a few days later Helga the cook had made Hot Pot for the family's evening meal according to Joe's secret recipe.

BONFIRE NIGHT.

ROBERT HAD FINISHED work in the municipal offices and was enjoying a quiet drink in the lounge bar. When he overheard Fred and The Colonel talking about the village bonfire, which was always held on some waste ground. Fred said "Well I am going to make a guy dressed in a old black suit and I Will put a blond wig on it. It will look like the Kaiser himself". Fred and the Colonel laughed. Robert against his better judgement said "Gustav does not understand our sense of humour, and he will be really upset if he sees a effigy of himself on the bonfire". Fred do not reply the matter was being brought up at the village hall where they were discussing the village bonfire.

Robert decided not to mention to Gustav about the meeting in the village hall he did not want Gustav upset. Gustav had plucked up the courage to write a letter to Gloria informing her that he was gay and Robert was his lover, and he hoped that they could still be good friends.

The evening of the meeting came round. The room was full, But Gustav was not there. The suggestion for the guy to be dressed up in a blond wig and black suit was raised. Robert expressed his opinion that Gustav would be hurt and that He did not understand our sense of humour. Fred could not understand what Robert was getting worked up about it was only a bit of fun. Then Gloria stood up Robert could see that she had not taken Gustav's letter well. "I will tell you why He is getting worked up Gustav Rothenburg is gay and Robert Thomas is his lover" Gloria said pointing to Robert. "Well I'll go to the foot of my stairs" said Fred. He was gob smacked. Red Maggie looked down cast you thought that she would have loved to use this information to attack Gustav with. Maggie said "I was looking forward to burning a effigy of the high and mighty Gustav Rothenburg, But now when everyone in the village learns that he's gay. People will only think it is because he's gay. There is no way I want people to think that of me. I would never oppose anyone because of their creed, gender or sexual orientation." Red Maggie said in her best public speaking voice. Then she turned to Robert saying "this does not mean that Ilike the high and mighty Kaiser and I Will not give up having a go at him". Robert thanked her and assured her that Gustav would understand. Fred too had gone off the idea he too did not want people to think that he was narrow minded. Fred said "the Kaiser's airs and graces rub him up the wrong way, but he would not go along with the idea of dressing the guy up in a black suit and blond wig now". Robert clearly wiping a rear from his eye thanked the meeting for their understanding.

Robert was in the Red Lion and he called Gustav to come for a drink. Gustav did not know of the reason but he felt like a drink and came along. When Gustav entered the bar it went quiet and some of the villagers turned and looked at him. Gustav knew something was amiss. Even Fred and the Colonel were nice to him. Joe asked Gustav what he wanted to drink. Gustav said to Joe "what's up ?" Robert came along side and explained that Gloria had told everyone about them and how Red Maggie had come to their aid as the defender of human rights. Robert explained that she had said that she did not like Gustav's ways but would not discriminate against him because of his sexuality. Robert and Gustav laughed together.

On bonfire night the whole village was there on the waste ground. The guy was not dressed up as the Kaiser. Gustav was standing near Robert unaware of what had taken place. Robert explained to the Rothenburgs the history of bonfire night. It still confused them, but it was an English custom so they respected it. Gustav was not keen on baked potatoes but he did like the homemade parkin. Gloria came up to them sheepishly and said that she was sorry for blurting out their secret. They understood why she had and how they were happy now the whole thing was out in the open. As the fire burnt down and the fireworks finished Robert, Gustav, Gloria and the family went to the Red Lion for a drink as usual.

WEIHNACHTEN
(CHRISTMAS)

ROBERT AND GUSTAV were having their weekly get together in the lounge bar of the Red Lion They had their favourite table in the corner. So they could see everyone who came in. It was early in December, and it would be the Rothenburgs first Christmas in Westhampton. Robert was eager to know what Gustav and his parents were doing. Gustav replied that uncle Ernst who owned the vineyard in Bad Rothenburg and his aunt Helga were coming to stay for Christmas. They were both Gustav's Godparents.

Gustav then told Robert how as a child he had gone into the kitchen and seen the Cook making the gingerbread Christmas decorations to hang on the tree., and how he and the other boys had to dress up as kings and each carrying a star go around the village carol singing. Gustav laughed at the happy memory. It was the last part of the conversation

Fred and The Colonel overheard. "So that's where he gets his grand ideas from. Being made to dress up as a king every year it's enough to turn any lads mind". They both laughed.

Gustav explained to Robert that in Germany they do not put presents under the tree. And it is Christkindl not Father Christmas who brings the presents. His presents would be put in a locked room and then at midnight on Christmas eve Vati and Mutti (Dad and Mum)would take him to the locked room open it and there was the tree all lit up with the presents on small tables. Gustav went silent for a moment and then said Ruefully "it's not the same as you get older is it". Robert told him to stop being so miserable and get another round in. But Robert did want to make the Rothenburgs first Christmas in Westhampton a special one. One to make them feel at home.

Westhampton high Street was illuminated by Christmas lights every year, and the Council were meeting tomorrow to decide which village personality would have the honour of switching on the lights. Robert guessed that they would opt for Gustav, But he was too obvious. He was at the Municipal offices so much he was almost a member of staff. No Gustav was too obvious. Then Robert came up with the perfect choice. He would reveal the name of the person at tomorrows meeting. Next day at the Municipal Buildings the Council was meeting. Robert attended all these meetings as a high ranking local Government worker to advise them. The subject of who was going to switch on the Christmas lights came up, and sure enough Gustav's name quickly came up. So Robert said he understood why they had thought of Gustav, but he was too obvious a choice. Why did they not consider Hildegard Rothenburg. The Councillors thought the matter over for a while and then agreed she would be a splendid choice. After the meeting Robert telephoned Gustav at his office, Jane answered the call and told Gustav that Robert was calling from the Municipal Offices. Robert told Gustav the good news. Gustav was delighted as both Uncle Ernst and Aunt Helga would be here then. The whole family could see the lights switched on and have a drink with Robert in the Red Lion and then afterwards Robert was also invited to a formal black tie Dinner in the drawing room at the Manor House.

So not only did the village decorate the high street. The various shops erected Christmas Trees. Joe had a tree up in the Lounge Bar of The Red Lion. Outside the municipal offices which was across the village green from the Red Lion. A small stage had been erected for the ceremony of switching on the Christmas lights. The ceremony would take place at six o'clock. At half past five the familiar sight of the big black Daimler pulled up near the stage closely followed by another car, which contained Uncle Ernst and Aunt Helga. After they had all got out of their cars Robert guided them to the party of Councillors on the stage. Fred and the Colonel were watching from outside the Red Lion. So they asked Joe who the visitors were. Joe explained that they were Gustav's relatives from Bad Rothenburg. Fred groaned "what even more Rothenburgs".

Then the Public address system sprang into life. The Leader of the Council addressed the crowd saying that they had welcomed the Rothenburgs into village of Westhampton and how everyone had made them feel welcome. And how much they had become part of the village especially Gustav. Fred turned to the Colonel and uttered "The man's a creep". Then the leader of the Council invited Hildegard to switch on the Christmas Lights. Even Fred and the Colonel could not disapprove of her. Then with a flash of light the whole high Street burst into life. And everyone shouted "hurrah".

The whole village had gone out of it's way to make the Rothenburgs feel at home. Jane had told Gloria about the gingerbread Christmas decorations Gustav knew as a child. So she had made some to serve in the Old Tea Shoppe and she had given a box to Gustav for the family. Joe had bought some bottles of gluewein from the supermarket in the nearest large town. And was serving it in the Red Lion. So when the family came into the lounge bar there was a glass of gluewein for everyone and Rev Jeremy Browne and the school had been teaching the Children to sing Silent night in German. So in the lounge bar the angelic looking Children sang Stille Nacht. Well with the warm gluewein and hearing stille Nacht Hildegard wept. She often gave the image of the tough old matriarch but beneath the surface she was a kind gentle person. And all these things going on reminded her of back home in Bad Rothenburg.

Then after a few drinks the party including Robert went back to the Manor House for the formal black tie Dinner in honour of Uncle Ernst and Aunt Helga. Gustav's relatives enjoyed the Manor House and Westhampton so much that they stayed until New Year and promised to make visiting their family in Westhampton a regular Holiday to see their family in England.

The meal was held in the drawing room and there was a Christmas Tree in the corner. The table had crisp white tablecloths on it and Candle decorations. After the meal the others went to go into the family's living room leaving Robert and Gustav alone together. Robert said he had another English Christmas tradition and pulled out a sprig of Mistletoe from his jacket pocket and kissed Gustav on the lips. Robert said "your coming to the village has been wonderful for me I Love you and you know that" Gustav blushed and said "yes I do" Then Robert kissed Gustav even longer and said "Merry Christmas and a happy new Year".

MR AND MRS THOMAS ?

IT WAS EARLY in the new year when Robert and Gustav asked to speak to his parents in their family's private quarters. Helmut and Hildegard had a good idea what was coming. Gustav and Robert stood before them in the wood panelled room before the large open fire place. Robert spoke for them both. Gustav and He had decided that they wanted to enter a civil partnership on the 14th of February.

Hildegard was silent for a moment and the silence was deafening. Then the old Matriarch said that first there were some important issues to be resolved. She did not want the Rothenburg wealth involved in the event that the relationship did not last.

And Robert would have to move into the Manor House there was ample room and he could rent out his home again just in case the relationship did not last. Then the really big issue Children whether by adoption or other means would have to be brought up as Rothenburgs. They were going to be her grandchildren. Robert did not want any of the Rothenburg wealth and Gustav did not want any of Robert's house so the answer was a legally binding agreement had to be signed before the day itself. So once all this was agreed the happy parents opened the champagne and invited Robert into the family.

Hildegard was well aware that the Church did not regard Civil Partnerships as weddings. But she was determined to push it as far as she could. For her this was going to be her son's wedding and Westhampton was going to remember it for a long while afterwards. It was going to be a Rothenburg wedding with all the trappings involved. So she said in her Matriarchal voice "Gustav Leopold and Robert Clive Jane and I and Gloria will organise this wedding Westhampton will remember the day my son got married".

The stag night well as Gustav was there as well it must have been the hen party also was held in the Lounge bar of the Red Lion. Joe had laid on a buffet. Robert and Gustav were there as was Helmut. Robert's parents had come along as had his brother Francis. There were some work colleagues of Robert's and some of the Councillors as well. Fred and the Colonel did not know quite what to make of this evening but the drinks were free so they joined in.

Hildegard, Jane and Gloria were the wedding sub committee. Hildegard wanted to thank the village for making the family welcome and so was going to involve as many of the villagers in the wedding as she could. Gloria was going to make the Wedding cake. Jane would ensure all the invitations and order of service sheets were printed. Joe was going to prepare the catering and run the Beer tent to be held in the grounds of the Manor House on the day.

The legal documents for the civil partnership would be signed at the Municipal offices and then it would be straight to St Marks for the blessing. Hildegard wanted her son's union to be blest by God. Then the wedding breakfast would be in the grand ballroom at the Manor House.

Jane sent out all the invitations of course to Uncle Ernst and Aunt Helga in Bad Rothenburg and to Roberts family. He had a relation in wales who was resigned to him marrying a nice English lad So Robert was overjoyed to tell him he was going to marry a German. Uncle Ernst and the rest of the Rothenburg Clan came in their black motors a few days before Valentine's day. So there would be plenty of Cars on the day. Robert's family were staying at the Red Lion and they heard all about the Kaiser there. But were pleasantly surprised Gustav was not as bad as some painted him.

The big day came Gerhardt woke Gustav as usual at seven with his cup of coffee. But today the usually calm Gustav was a bag of nerves. Gerhardt took him in hand and had him follow his normal routine. The hired morning suit was laid out. All the men had agreed to wear the same outfit. A Black tailed coat, Striped morning trousers, light grey Gloves and a light Grey top Hat. But Gustav had insisted that they all wear a ostentatious waistcoat. Gustav had breakfast and then Helmut, Gustav and Uncle Ernst entered the Daimler to go to the Municipal Offices for nine forty five. There already were Robert, His brother Francis, Jane and Gloria. After the civil partnership ceremony was completed they headed for St Marks for the blessing. The Vicar had stressed that in the eyes of the Church a civil partnership was not the same as a wedding. Well Hildegard was going to make it a close run thing. There were flowers decorating the sides of the pews. And Robert and Gustav would process down the Aisle to Pachbel's Canon and have the hymn love divine all loves excelling. Rev Browne would read from St Paul's first Epistle to the Corinthians Chapter thirteen on love and gave a short homily. The Choir sang Ave Maria. Then the couple processed out of the Church to the arrival of the Queen of Sheba. Red Maggie said "The Kaiser's more like the Queen of Westhampton". Fred and The Colonel laughed. Outside the Church the guests threw confetti over the happy couple and Gloria managed to get a kiss of Gustav. Heinrich opened the doors of the black Daimler to let the happy couple get in. The Daimler had white ribbons on it and the tin cans at the back with the sign just married on it.

The Cavalcade of Rothenburg Motors headed for the Manor House. The Wedding sub committee had been working overtime. The Ballroom was formally set out with tables covered in white tablecloths each place had a place card decorated with the family's coat of Arms. Hildegard had arranged for the happy couple to enter the ballroom from the terrace via a archway of Roses. There was a string quartet providing back ground music during the meal. The Wine was all from Uncle Ernst vineyard of course. Robert and Gustav were in the Centre with the respective parents either side. When Helmut spoke about Robert and Gustav. Gustav pretended he had something in his eye as he wept. And when Robert told them of how they had met.

Then with all the formalities out of the way. The tables were pushed back and the beer tent on the gardens was opened. And the informal party went into full swing. Gustav and Robert decided to be magnanimous and invite Fred, The Colonel and Red Maggie Pettigrew. Well Jane's Mother liked Gustav so to invite her they had to invite the rest. The list to dance with Gustav was long. Jane, Gloria, and Jane's Mother. But Robert managed to have the first dance with Gustav. Fred still thought it a might odd two blokes dancing together, but the beer was free.

The women had all dressed in new outfits. They made sure no one wore the same outfit as the other, and Hildegard had a large grand brand new hat. She said that she was the bride's Mother so it was expected. The beer tent proved a popular idea. Most of the Village was there in the grounds of the Manor. The terrace had fairy lights strung along it. The party music was played by a D J from the village. Gloria had now accepted that she was never going to steal Gustav's heart. Gerhardt the faithful family servant was pleased to see Gustav so happy.

Hildegard had been true to her word She had made sure that the village would remember her son's wedding for a long time to come. The whole affair was a grand showy event with the party going on into the early hours of the morning.

Robert did not know if it was politically correct to refer to it as a honeymoon, But a few days later on He had arranged for him and Gustav to go to the Maldives. In a quiet bungalow by the shore. So that they could sunbathe and swim. But that was in a few days time. Now Robert and a slightly drunk Gustav went up the grand staircase. Robert opened the door to the bedroom which was now their room. He picked Gustav up and carried him over the threshold before both of them collapsed upon the bed in laughter. So the new Mr and Mrs Thomas had their first night together as a legally joined couple. Hildegard and Helmut as any other parents had wept as there son got married. They were not following the scruples of the Church as far as they were concerned their son was getting married and it would be a day to remember in the village.

Hildegard had tried to ensure that as many of the villagers had participated in this civil partnership. And its celebration. The whole village had come together to wish Robert and Gustav all the best for the future. Even Fred, The Colonel and Red Maggie could not find fault with that.

MARRIED LIFE

GUSTAV AND ROBERT had a honeymoon to remember in the Maldives, but now it was back to Westhampton. And life as a couple. Gustav enjoyed having Robert near him in the bedroom. But for Robert there was a problem. Gustav stil had breakfast with his family just as though nothing had changed. Robert felt uncomfortable kissing Gustav or holding his hand with his parents around. He was reluctant to kiss Gustav goodbye before they both went to work. They had to shower and come down stairs fully dressed the Rothenburgs were too formal for the Robert's habit of lounging around at weekends in nothing but a bathrobe and your underwear.

So it was not long before they had their first row and it was about the family having breakfast together. Gustav could not understand Robert's objections. But Robert wanted those moments to be romantic with Gustav and with the in laws around. His passion was gone. Gustav's parents were having breakfast on the terrace. When they heard the raised voices in the drawing room. As Gustav became angry he lapsed into his native German. So Robert had to tell him to calm down and speak English. Robert decided to skip breakfast and go straight to the office. Gustav went out onto the terrace despite his best efforts Hildegard could see he was upset. "We told you it would not be easy" she said. "What was your first row about?" Helmut asked in a fatherly way. Gustav explained the problem as best he could, But Gustav could not see a problem. Helmut said that Robert wants to spend some time with you alone and I guess he feels it difficult with the in laws around. Hildegard said that she would try to think of a solution. But in the meantime Gustav should not worry everything would turn out alright. Robert came home late opting for another drink in the Red Lion. Gustav was pacing up and down wondering why he was so late. Dinner that evening in the drawing room was a tense affair. Finally Hildegard snapped "Look you two you cannot keep sulking over your row. Let's find a solution". Robert explained that he loved being with the family, but there were times when he wanted time alone with Gustav. Hildegard thought for a moment and suggested a compromise that they only all met together for breakfast at the weekends. Gustav was torn emotionally between his parents and his partner. Try as they might to organise a timetable for breakfast it was difficult for relationships do not run to timetables.

Gerhardt did not mind waking the happy couple up in the morning at seven with a cup of coffee for Gustav and a cup of tea for Robert. Gerhardt had looked after Gustav since he was a lad. Gerhardt had been Gustav's barber for many years and still trimmed his hair. So he was pleased to see Gustav happy. Robert too was getting used to the idea of having ones clothes laid out for you in the morning. The long term solution to the breakfast problem was if all the family was present they would have breakfast in the drawing room. If it was only Helmut and Hildegard they had breakfast in their private quarters.

Gustav and Robert had just had their first row. Gustav said that Robert was not talking to one of his office juniors now. Robert called Gustav petulant. But now the row was behind them and they were in love once more.

Hildegard watched her tv programmes. In the past Helmut would go to the wine cellars to check up on his beloved wine bottles. But now with Robert here in the Manor. Helmut felt he did not have to endure the programmes any more He asked Robert and Gustav if they wanted to go to the Red Lion for a drink. They agreed and so the boys night out came into being. They went to the Red Lion and had Robert's and Gustav's favourite table in the lounge. Joe was delighted with the extra custom and curious to see how

Robert and Gustav were settling down. Fred and the Colonel referred to them as Mr and Mrs Kaiser.

Hildegard was not to be out done. If the boys were going out. She would invite the girls in. So the girls night in was born. She invited Jane and Gloria around to the Manor for Sherry. Gloria baked some cakes for them, and they would gossip or watch old soppy films. Robert had followed Hildegard's advice and put his house up for rent to a local family. In order to do so he had coaxed Gustav into mowing his front lawn. Gustav was horrified what was Robert trying to do to him But he rather enjoyed the novelty of mowing a lawn. But only the once though.

Councillor Red Maggie was going through the Council's rule book to see if there was a regulation preventing your partner from being on the same sub committee as you at the same time. She was not successful. Robert knew that she would not be. It was his job to make sure the Councillors stayed within the rules. Jane noticed that Gustav was trying to make Robert dress more adventurously and Gustav was more relaxed married life was good for him. The boys night out gave a whole new lease of life to Helmut. Robert had his brother Francis come to the Manor for weekends and holidays. And Robert's parents became firm friends with Helmut and Hildegard. So married life had started for Gustav and Robert and now they had their first row, but also learned to kiss and make up.

GOD MOVES IN MYSTERIOUS WAYS

HAVE YOU HAD that feeling that you were destined to be somewhere, and just how small the world is. Robert had rented out his house to a local family George Watkins and his wife Sheila and their two twin boys Billy and Bobby Watkins. Although the boys were not identical twins. George was a qualified gardener. But along the way he had acquired other skills. He could put his hand to joinery or plumbing. He was out of work at the moment, But he was actively seeking another post.

Gustav and Robert had gone off to a tourism sub committee meeting at the Municipal Buildings. There was a strict division of labour at the Manor House Gustav was finance, Helmut a true Rothenburg had wine in his blood, and so he was quality control. He made sure all the wine that went to the Red lion was of the best quality.

Hildegard was personnel. She did the hiring and firing. So she was interviewing candidates for the vacant post of gardener. George Watkins was appointed. George had two eight year old boys and he asked Hildegard if she did not mind if he brought them along at weekends and during the holidays. He would make sure that they did not get in the way. When Gustav and Robert came home around teatime. They noticed a stranger pushing a wheelbarrow across the grounds towards the greenhouses at the back of the Manor. The stranger spotted Robert and said "Hello Mr Thomas" Robert realised it was George Watkins who he had rented his house to. George introduced himself to Gustav. They would soon find out that George would soon be invaluable to the Manor. On the first day George had brought sandwiches from home for his lunch. But Helga the Rothenburg's cook said that she made more than enough food for the family So George had a hot meal in the kitchen Well the vegetables which he grew in the greenhouses ended up there it seemed only right.

George brought the boys with him at weekends and in the holidays So it was soon a common sight to see Billy and Bobby Watkins around the Manor House. They were not naughty boys. But sometimes they let their curiosity get the better of them. So soon it was Uncle Helmut and Aunt Hildegard. But never Uncle Gustav. He was not the avuncular type. He remained the Kaiser behind his back.

But Billy and Bobby boasted at school that they could call the Kaiser Gustav.

The boys loved helping Heinrich wash and repair the Daimler, But they were really fascinated when he took it to bits to service. They would help clean the parts and they were never happier than when they were dirty. Once after helping Heinrich he and they came into Helga's kitchen covered in oil. She was besides herself. But once she had them clean up She gave them some cakes. Heinrich told the boys that after he had given the Daimler a service he liked to give it a little run to make sure it was in working order and would they like to come with him. Well it was not long before those two scamps were in the back of the Daimler pretending to be Gustav. They waved at everyone along the high street. As they passed by in the big black car. Then at St Mark's Heinrich turned the car around and turning to the boys said "now what does Master Gustav say now" Billy and Bobby replied in unison "Heinrich Nach Hause Bitte" They all laughed and Heinrich thought they were amusing.

Once Gustav spotted the boys coming out of the kitchen eating cakes. Helga would never change. She had spoiled him with cakes as a boy just the same. If the boys hurt themselves at the Manor it was Helga who supplied the plasters, the ointment, and tender loving care. Robert noticed the boys playing on the grand staircase coming down it as Gustav with all his arrogance. Robert stayed hidden, But he had to laugh who was it who said imitation is the sincerest form of flattery.

Helmut would not allow the boys in his precious wine cellars. He kept them locked. It was the twins who had given Hildegard the idea that the Rothenburgs should have a basket of fruit and vegetables in the harvest festival at St Mark's. They had learned about it at school and they had told Hildegard all about it. So it was only right that the two boys should hae the honour of carrying the large basket at the harvest Festival.

George could repair leaking pipes, fix doors, as well as tend the gardens. So it was not long before he became George the indispensable. Billy and Bobby could be seen climbing trees, pushing empty wheelbarrows around, and carrying the smaller tools. But they brought out the maternal side in Hildegard. She liked having them around. They brought life back into the Manor. Jane found them invaluable for carrying parcels or running messages in the Manor.

Robert renting out his house to the Watkins had brought a valuable member of staff to the Manor House. And the boys with their love for life were a breathe of fresh air. They were never happier then when they were watching Heinrich repair the Daimler or help their Father in the greenhouses planting seeds in the soil. And getting mucky. As well as visiting Helga in the kitchen knowing just when she would have some home made cakes hot from the oven. They liked being on the high street and they saw the black Daimler and Gustav got out. They would shout to Gustav, and he would turn and acknowledge them. Then people would turn and look at them and think who are they that they can call the Kaiser Gustav. But the adventures of Billy and Bobby Watkins are only just beginning.

THE PAST IS
ALWAYS WITH US

As I Said the adventures of Billy and Bobby Watkins were only just beginning. But where do I Begin with what happened next. It was a quiet sunny day and the twins were playing in the grounds of the Manor House near to the stream that was the boundary of the Rothenburg land. When they noticed a large piece of metal protruding from a overgrown mound. They peered at it closely but thankfully they did not disturb it. They called their Father George the gardener to come and see what they had found. When George noticed the tail section he became worried and informed Gustav of his suspicions. The Police were called to the Manor and when they saw the device. They called the Bomb Disposal Unit. It was a five hundred pound German second world war Bomb. Robert saw the irony in the situation a German Bomb found on land owned by the Rothenburgs. Gustav knew that Fred and the Colonel in the Red Lion would also find it highly amusing.

The Police sealed off the area. The local Constable was only too aware of how embarrassed Gustav found the whole situation. The twins asked the Bomb squad if they were going to detonate the Bomb there and then. The Officers had to disappoint them. The device would be defused and taken away. The Bomb squad guessed the German second World War bomber had been heading for the nearby large town, which was heavily bombed in the war and had released it's load early.

The local newspaper the Westhampton Gazette sent along a reporter. They did not have a good working relationship with the family and especially Gustav when they had reported that his behaviour was from a bygone era, and he still expected people to bow down to the Lord of the Manor. The only contact the paper had was through Jane Wright. She had given them a decent photograph of Gustav for their articles. The journalist asked Gustav if he could not see the humour of a German Bomb being found on their land. Gustav said that he could not understand the question and that the interview was over.

But Gustav's gut instinct about how the press would report the incident were well founded. The paper had banner headlines "German UXB found on Rothenburg land, and it did not get any better in the Red Lion that evening when

Gustav was having a drink with his Father Helmut, and Robert in the lounge bar. Fred and The Colonel spotted him from the other bar. They shouted over to him "Gustav was there a Luftwaffe Airfield near Bad Rothenburg in the second World War only the Police said that the Bomb they found had made in Bad Rothenburg on it". Gustav fumed but did not reply. The Colonel continued "You know you could tell a Bomb made in Bad Rothenburg it made a whining noise as it came down". They both laughed. Gustav had heard enough "you two are not very funny my family make wine not Bombs." They realised that they had got under Gustav's skin. So They were not going to ease up. "Gustav what did your family do in the War?". But this time it was Helmut who responded "We do not talk about such things in Germany. But our vineyards suffered badly in the War, and it took many years for the business to recover. Now Joe the Landlord decided that there had been enough Kaiser baiting for one night.

The Twins were disappointed they were looking forward to a big bang. But Helga the cook thought that they had been very brave and deserved some cakes. The Twins had their picture in the local paper near the site of the Bomb. And they were treated like heroes in their class at school.

Gustav could not understand Fred and the Colonel making fun of the incident with the Bomb. Gustav was only too aware that for some Villagers Germany and the

War were not to far apart. And the Bomb had brought back painful memories for his parents. Gustav was trying to get the Locals in Westhampton to appreciate the family for their wines. So the Bomb was a unhelpful reminder. But he need not have worried the Bomb was a nine day wonder, and was soon forgotten. Besides Gustav and his arrogance still gave Fred and the Colonel plenty of ammunition for Kaiser baiting. They knew that they could easily wind Gustav up. Robert tried to get him to relax and not to respond to their jibes in the Red Lion. But he could not. He had to tell them what he thought of them and their poor humour. But for Fred and the Colonel Gustav in one of his teutonic tantrums was a comical sight. But for Robert and Joe it was just another day at the office the banter between Gustav, Fred and the Colonel.

I feel like Dr Watson recording the exploits of Sherlock Holmes in these stories of Gustav. By the way Gustav says see you soon.